Enchanted by the Highlander

ENCHANTED BY THE HIGHLANDER

A GUARDIANS OF THE ISLES ROMANCE

GERRI RUSSELL

TULE
PUBLISHING

DEDICATION

This novel, born from my imagination and fueled by countless cups of tea, is dedicated to my husband, my sons, and my daughters. You are all an unwavering source of inspiration and joy.

And to my readers, may these pages transport you to realms unknown, ignite your curiosity, and remind you that magic exists even in the mundane. As you read, know that every word carries a piece of my heart.

PROLOGUE

London, England
Thursday, April 18th, 1743

"COME NOW, ROSALYN," Lieutenant Long said, his wide grey eyes pleading with her for a small boon. "I am leaving for Scotland tonight, and I would take a kiss from you to keep me company on the frigid Scottish nights."

In the morning light, Rosalyn de Clare looked around the small London park. Her gaze shifting from their horses, grazing on tendrils of fresh spring grass at the base of a tree to beyond, where fashionable men and women strolled along the path. "I would not want to cause a scandal."

"One kiss. After all the attention I have given you as of late, it is at least my due." He grabbed her waist and pulled her towards him.

Rosalyn struggled in his arms. "I did not ask you to pay any particular attention to me. Please, James, release me now before someone sees us."

"Everyone on the path has moved on. No one is near at present." Lieutenant Long's gaze shifted from her face to the parted edges of her collar before descending to where the

GERRI RUSSELL

fabric of her riding habit moulded over her breast.

Heat flooded Rosalyn's cheeks. "Truly, James, you must release me," she said tartly, starting to feel very uncomfortable with how alone they were behind the ancient oak tree. She never should have agreed to come with him on this outing without a maid or a footman.

He shifted closer, and Rosalyn's heart jammed in her throat. His mouth descended towards hers. His hand drifted from her waist to the nape of her neck. Instead of fear, curiosity flared. She had never kissed a man before. His lips were hard as they slid against her lips, claiming her, marking her as his.

Uncertain of what to do with her hands, she left them to dangle at her sides as the kiss became harder, more insistent. It was then that she felt an unaccountable prickle of alarm scratch down her spine. She brought her hands up and pushed hard against James's chest when a hot, hard part of him pressed against her. He gripped her arms and with one hand, tried to shove her down, while the other hand fumbled with the fall of his trousers.

For an instant, Rosalyn was paralysed by shock and fear, until a spark of rage erupted inside her. She twisted her shoulders, trying to free herself from his grip, but instead of freedom, his fingers dug into the fabric of her gown. The sleeve tore, exposing her shoulder.

Lust filled his gaze as his hand slipped from her shoulder to cup her partly exposed breast.

"No!" This man wanted more than a kiss from her. Rosalyn jerked her knee upward with furious strength, and she landed a blow to the most vulnerable part of him. His eyes flared as he howled and jerked back. She pulled out of his arms, her heart racing.

"What in heaven's name is going on here?"

Rosalyn's breath hitched as she looked to the left, horrified to see that what she had hoped to have been a private moment, was seen by none other than the Duchess of Leeds and several ladies and gentlemen in her company.

James, recovering far more quickly than Rosalyn, smiled at the great lady then nodded, as though nothing untoward had just happened. "Good day, Your Grace."

The duchess returned the lieutenant's smile, but when she turned to Rosalyn, her eyes narrowed with disdain. "Scandalous behaviour. Your brother will not be pleased."

Rosalyn clutched the torn edges of her gown, trying to conceal her exposed flesh. Her heart pounded in her ears. The world swam before her eyes as she swayed on her feet.

"I should have expected such behaviour from you," the duchess continued to berate her. Behind that woman, Rosalyn could hear the swelling of whispers that rippled on the morning breeze. Unable to bear their comments a moment longer, she forced her dizziness away and darted to her horse, jumped up onto the saddle, then fled past the startled, staring duchess and her friends.

Her heart thundering in her chest the entire journey

home, Rosalyn raced to her room, locked the door, then buried her head in her pillows. Why had she ever agreed to go to the park with Lieutenant Long today? And why had she not run away when he had asked her for a kiss? Rosalyn knew, without a doubt, that whatever events happened next would not bode well for her.

Three hours later, she was summoned to the library by her brother. Upon entering the chamber, she saw his eyes narrow with annoyance and her stomach sank. She sat in the chair across from his desk. "You wished to see me?" Rosalyn tried to keep her voice from trembling.

"You have humiliated me to the depths of my soul with your wanton behaviour in the park today," Hugh de Clare said brusquely.

"Hugh, I—"

"I do not want to hear your excuses. You played fast and loose and now you must suffer the consequences."

"No, Hugh. You do not understand—"

His fist came crashing down against the table. "No, it is you who does not understand. You are ruined. Beyond repair. All of London is gossiping about your little indiscretion, and as a result I have done the only thing I can."

"Which is?" Rosalyn tried to gather her wits, to find a way to reach through her brother's anger, to the young man who had raised her since the death of their parents.

"I have acted within my rights as your guardian," he bit out as his face flushed. "I've convinced Lieutenant Long that it is in his best interest to marry you, immediately."

"You what?" she gasped, clutching the arms of the chair to control her shaking.

Her brother did not seem to notice or, more likely, did not care. "The only concession the military man asked was that you meet him in Scotland for the ceremony because his regiment was heading north forthwith." Hugh narrowed his gaze on her. "You have two days to pack your things. I have arranged for several of my finest men to accompany you on your journey north."

"Why are you doing this, Hugh?" Rosalyn asked with a shimmer of tears in her eyes, trying to understand her brother's persistent cruelty to her. "I have done everything you ever asked of me, all while trying not to be an imposition."

He stared past her at the wall with blank indifference. "I have asked Miss Amelia Jenkins to marry me, and she has accepted on the condition that she would not have to share this house with you. So, this arrangement with Lieutenant Long is auspicious for both of us. You will have a husband, and I will no longer be responsible for you when I take a wife."

Rosalyn swallowed hard, trying to force back the tears that fell onto her cheeks. "Is there anything I can do to make you change your mind?"

"Not a damn thing," Hugh bit out. "The arrangements have been made. You will join Lieutenant Long in Scotland in two days' time."

CHAPTER ONE

Dunvegan Castle, Isle of Skye, Scotland
Saturday, April 20th, 1743

A S THE SUN set in the window behind him, Keiran MacLeod moved to the door of his chamber, hesitating for a moment. This evening marked that it had been a fortnight since he'd returned to Dunvegan Castle and his clan. He drew a tight breath. And every day since, his marriage-minded sisters and sisters-in-law had been parading at least one local lady before him with the hopes that she would catch his eye.

Tonight, he was certain they would bring forth Arabella, Gwendolyn's sixteen-year-old sister, as a potential mate. At least that was what Gwendolyn, his brother Alastair's wife, had intimated early in the day. Drawing a fortifying breath, he stepped from the chamber and was met by his sister Rowena.

"There you are. I was just coming up to look for you," Rowena said. The fact that she had been leaning against the wall belied her statement. She'd been waiting for him to emerge. "What took you so long?" Her dark eyes narrowed.

It gave him a start every time how much Rowena looked like their mother. Dark hair, dark eyes, but with a kindness that seemed to shine from within. "I had a little trouble with my tartan." It was a partial truth and as good an excuse as any for why he had lingered in his chamber so long.

"Come." Rowena looped her arm through his, trying to pull him forward. "Arabella waits in the great hall for you."

Keiran remained where he stood, resisting. Stolen by the fairies as a child, he'd been magically aged from only a month old to three and twenty by the fairy king who had no liking for infants. Oberon had aged him maturity-wise as well, though at times he still felt childlike in that he wanted to rage sometimes against all that had happened to him. He was a fairy, yet he was human. He belonged to two different families, two different worlds. His human family wanted so much for him to be like them, to pretend he'd never left them. But he had. He'd been a fairy for a while. Could he ever fully leave that part of himself behind and be the MacLeod they wanted?

Every day he tried to adjust to his new life among not only his kin, but also humans and their strange ways, such as why all the women of the castle seemed to want him to marry before he even figured out who he truly was in this realm. "Why are all of you so eager to see me wed?"

Rowena's features fell. "We simply want you to be happy."

"Wouldn't I be happier if I was allowed to choose a bride

myself? And in my own time?" he asked.

"It is just that since you've returned you have been so aloof, so sullen. I know all of us and this castle are unfamiliar to you, but we . . ." Rowena's features pinched. "I want to see you settled or at least happy before Marcus and I leave on the morrow."

There was a long silence before Keiran spoke. "I have been away a long time. I need more than another evening to readjust to my new life. Please give me the freedom of discovery at my own pace without rushing me into marriage."

A pink tinge stained her cheeks. "But—"

"Sail off with Marcus to follow your dreams, Rowena. Mine will be found elsewhere and on my own time."

She nodded. "You cannot blame a sister for trying."

"I am more than certain Gwendolyn, Fiona, Isolde, and Aria will continue in your absence," he said with a hint of humour.

She smiled as she shrugged. "You are on your own there, for I will be gone soon." Her smile faded. "You may have been absent from Dunvegan Castle for nine years, but we all love you and only want what is best for you."

"I can appreciate that, but I am still trying to reconcile my present with my past and learn how to be a human among humans."

Rowena placed her hand against Keiran's chest. "No matter where you have been or what has happened in the past, you are a MacLeod and not so different from the rest of your family."

A jab of pain pierced his heart. If she only knew how different he was from everyone. "They accept me because they must, but I doubt any of you will ever truly understand me."

"Give it time, Keiran. It was hard for the MacLeods to accept Marcus and even Aria at first, but they finally did." Rowena offered him an encouraging smile. "Come along, we really must go to supper before the entire family comes looking for you."

He remained rooted to the floor. "Only if you promise there will be no more matchmaking tonight."

"I promise." Without waiting for a response, she took his hand and dragged him down the stairs to the great hall. As expected, he had barely set foot in the chamber before Arabella was paraded before him.

"Good evening, Keiran," Gwendolyn greeted at the doorway with one of her twin infants in her arms and Arabella at her side. "Might you sit with us tonight?"

Keiran offered the young girl a bow before tossing Gwendolyn an irritated scowl.

Rowena shook her head. "I promised Keiran a night free of entanglements," she said as she continued escorting him past the pink-cheeked young woman. "Perhaps after a night spent talking about books with Orrick, battle techniques with Tormod, or the affairs of the estate with Alastair, he will be receptive of feminine companionship once again."

Rowena finally released his arm as she approached the head table where his three eldest brothers—along with Graeme and Marcus—were seated. A large hand-drawn map was spread across the table before them. "I will leave you to your fate." With a wink, she turned to rejoin Gwendolyn and Arabella.

"What was that all about?" Orrick asked, patting an open space on the bench beside him.

"A desperate attempt by Rowena to make me feel contrite for not falling into the plans your wives have for my future," Keiran said as he slid onto the bench.

"You are safe with us," Orrick said, his voice filled with affection as he clapped Keiran on the shoulder.

Alastair, his eldest brother and laird of their clan, poured then passed Keiran a mug of ale. He accepted it gratefully as he glanced at the men beside him. Next to his brothers sat Marcus, Rowena's husband, and Graeme, Aria's husband. Their faces were still unfamiliar, but their welcoming smiles were not. These men had been nothing but kind to Keiran since his arrival. They had walked him through every part of the estate, had battled with him in the lists—not going easy on him—for which he was thankful. That he had to work to succeed helped him feel a sense of accomplishment.

"Are you finding your way around the estate well enough?" Tormod asked.

Keiran sipped his ale then nodded. "Aye. I spend most of my days wandering around, since I have little else to do.

Today I found a place on the northern side of the castle where the three of you—Alastair, Tormod, and Orrick—carved your initials into the stone."

"I had forgotten about that." Alastair laughed as supper was served.

Mrs Honey's dinner was a simple affair. A fine stew of beef and vegetables braised in ale, with thick slices of yeasty bread, and more ale to wash it all down. When they had all finished, they returned their attention to Keiran.

"Are you feeling more at home?" Alastair asked.

Keiran raised his gaze to Alastair from the map that he had studied all through the meal. "I would feel more at ease if I had something to do besides surveying the estate. There must be some way I can contribute?"

"There is," Alastair said, glancing once more at the map. "You have proven yourself to be intelligent and resourceful since you arrived here. It is time for us to start including you in the MacLeod family affairs. I would like you to become my estate manager."

"Truly?" Keiran replied, his excitement growing.

"Aye. I shall go over each estate with you tomorrow and all the tasks managing them entails."

"Whatever I can do to help." Keiran smiled. Had his family finally accepted him for who he was? He had a history with the fairies, but the MacLeods did as well. For they all possessed a hint of fairy blood since the time four hundred years ago when Laird Iain Cair MacLeod married a fairy princess. Their child had passed down that trait to all the MacLeods since.

"I am glad you are willing to assist us because we need your help in an urgent matter. The threat of an English invasion grows daily," Tormod explained, drawing Keiran's attention back to the moment. "There are reports of the British army stationed here and here." Tormod pointed to two areas on the map well away from where Keiran presumed Dunvegan to be, based on the shape of the familiar coastline. "The English are sending more troops all the time, growing ever closer to the Isle of Skye. The clans are growing anxious."

Keiran frowned. "I understand that an English presence here in Scotland is not a welcome thing, but how can I help with that?"

"We want you to go with us tomorrow morning to retrieve the latest troop movement report from Clan Nicolson," Tormod said grimly. "The only way to keep the clans safe is to know where the English are positioning themselves. We have heard rumours of an impending attack on Scottish clans who are supporters of Charles Stuart returning to the throne of Scotland."

"I am overjoyed at being included in your plans, but do not all of you need to see Marcus and Rowena off on their journey tomorrow?" Keiran asked.

All gazes shifted to Marcus. The dark-haired man's features were pensive. "Rowena would be upset if her brothers were not there to bid her farewell, though I am also certain she would understand."

"If this mission is to be a stealthy one, then perhaps it is best if one man goes instead of a whole contingent. It would be far less conspicuous, and easier to manoeuvre within the cover of the landscape." Keiran pressed his lips together as he concentrated on the map. "Where is this meeting to take place?"

"Near Struan, along the west coast," Tormod replied with a tilt of his head.

"Where is Struan on the map?" Keiran asked.

"Are you ready for such a mission?" Tormod asked as he pointed to a location along the western coastline.

"Nay, 'tis too dangerous for you to go alone." Orrick's brows came tighter as he regarded Keiran. "Besides, you are still unfamiliar with the human realm."

Keiran flipped the map to hide it. "The west coast is approximately an hour's ride on horseback from Dunvegan, continuing south on to Struan would take perhaps another hour. There are multiple woodlands, and plenty of hills where I can stay hidden and assess the situation as I proceed on my way."

Alastair arched a brow. "How did you know all that?"

"I was always the scout sent out to assess conflicts between fairies in different regions of Fairyland. I learned how to read the landscape, judge distances, determine threats, and advised Oberon what actions to take."

That his brothers stared at him wide-eyed brought a flare of warmth to Keiran's chest. "Had you assumed I did nothing in Fairyland over the past nine years?"

Alastair recovered first and cast Keiran a contrite grin. "Forgive us. We are all still trying to reconcile that our baby brother is as old as we are and very skilled in certain things."

"Are you certain you are up for this task?" Orrick asked.

"Aye." Keiran straightened. "It seems simple enough."

"Nothing is simple when the English are involved. Remember that," Tormod said.

Keiran nodded.

Alastair looked to his brothers, then Marcus and Graeme. "It looks like we will all be here to see Marcus and Rowena off on their next journey." His gaze landed on Keiran. "And you, dear brother, will take your place as the new family spy."

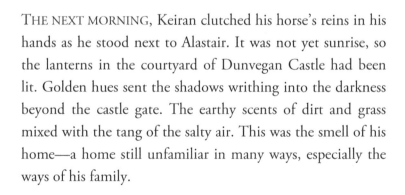

THE NEXT MORNING, Keiran clutched his horse's reins in his hands as he stood next to Alastair. It was not yet sunrise, so the lanterns in the courtyard of Dunvegan Castle had been lit. Golden hues sent the shadows writhing into the darkness beyond the castle gate. The earthy scents of dirt and grass mixed with the tang of the salty air. This was the smell of his home—a home still unfamiliar in many ways, especially the ways of his family.

Earlier abovestairs, determined to wear the clothing of his people, he had lain his clan's tartan on the floor, pleating it the way his brother Callum had shown him. It had taken Keiran three tries before he had managed to create something akin to the lay of the garments his brothers wore.

Despite the fact the garment was crafted from marvellously soft wool, the human-made cloth itched against his skin. It took great strength not to scratch his upper thighs as he slipped his feet into equally unfamiliar leather boots. These were the garments of his people. No matter how uncomfortable they were, he would wear them until they felt as though they were a part of who he was—the last-born son of a Scottish laird, not the favoured yet stolen son of the fairy king.

"Keiran, are you listening to me?" Alastair asked, bringing Keiran's attention back to the courtyard and the men beside him. "Perhaps you are not yet ready for this task."

Keiran straightened, terrified that his wandering thoughts might cost him the very thing he had sought since he'd returned: the trust of his family.

"Nay. I am ready. I can do this, Alastair. Please." He'd never had to beg for anything in the fairy realm. Oberon had allowed him anything he asked until the enchantment over him had been broken by his fairy sister, Aria. Then Oberon had called him a fool.

Keiran bristled at the memory. He was no fool and he would prove such to his kin. He needed them to look upon him not as a sad charity case who had lost his childhood, but as someone who could grasp his future and mould it to his liking. Keiran needed this simple task Alastair asked of him to prove to himself and to his family he was ready to be a man, not a youngling in the nursery. "I won't let you down."

"I know you won't." Alastair still hesitated, studying Keiran intensely. "Are you certain you want to do this mission alone? I could send a small contingent of soldiers to accompany you."

Keiran shook his head. "I will be less conspicuous as a single rider should I come upon the enemy." He could ride a horse, navigate the land better than most humans—having learned his navigating skills in Fairyland—and could hold his own in battle, making him the perfect choice for this mission. "A simple enough task even for me. I can do this, Alastair. Give me a chance to prove my worth."

Alastair nodded. "The Nicolsons will meet you past the village of Struan at the iron-age broch, Dun Beag. The meeting shall take place as the sun reaches its zenith, meaning you will be able to ride there and back well before sunset."

Keiran mounted the horse and turned towards the open gates. "Then I shall see you at supper."

The silence of morning surrounded Keiran as he passed through the gates, following the path to the south-east. With a renewed sense of determination, Keiran urged the horse beneath him into a faster gait as he watched a yellowish-white glow spread across the land before him. His breath hitched at the sight. He still could not believe the differences in the light between the human and fairy realms, especially at sunrise.

As the sun crested over the horizon, he felt his whole being warm, stretch, as though he too were embracing the new day that was upon him. As the crisp white light intensified, he drew in a slow breath, connecting momentarily with the source beyond his reach, the source of all life, hoping today would not be the day Oberon, the king of the fairies and his one-time father, would force him back to Fairyland.

Keiran turned to look behind him at the fading image of Dunvegan Castle. The MacLeods were happy to have him back, and he was eager to find his place among his human family. Yet, a part of him also held back, waiting for something to happen, for Oberon to show himself. The MacLeods assumed Keiran would be safe in the human realm forever because Oberon had vanished under a wave of fairy magic. But Keiran had witnessed Oberon's ability to survive when defeated previously. There would be a day in the future when the fairy king would reappear to take his revenge against both Keiran for leaving and the MacLeods for taking what Oberon believed was his—both Keiran and the magical Fairy Flag.

Keiran sighed as he pulled his thoughts back to the present. Perhaps he should have told his brothers about the possibility of Oberon returning, but Keiran hadn't wanted anything to stand in the way of his going on this mission for his clan. It might take years for Oberon to retaliate. Or he may never come for the MacLeods again. Instead of dwelling on what might happen someday, Keiran watched the morning light illuminate the leaves and branches of the trees with a gentle caress. The trees welcomed the light, stretching their limbs and swaying in the breeze. With a second sigh, Keiran encouraged his horse into a gallop, feeling suddenly alone and longing for something he could not name.

As he rode, the bright and fresh morning light came over the landscape ahead of him, changing the colours and shapes of everything it touched. The green grass and the rusty-gold moss that covered the moorland looked more alive and vibrant than anything he had ever seen in Fairyland.

Two hours later, Keiran held the reins loosely in his hands as he navigated the unkempt road leading into Struan. Instead of entering the village, he headed for the grassy terrain along the outskirts, not wanting to bring any attention to himself. He continued, pausing only for a small herd of deer to bolt across his path and disappear into the sparse woodland on the other side.

When finally, he came to the top of a ridge, he peered into the distance, seeing the broch. Keiran frowned. The iron-age fort had seen better days. The roof had collapsed, and the stones of the once mighty tower lay in crumbles about its base. He had assumed the Nicolsons resided here, but clearly, he had been wrong. No one could live in such a derelict place.

Keiran rode down the hillside until he pulled his horse to a halt in front of the ruined doorway, then jumped down. Allowing his horse to graze on the grass nearby, he walked along the overgrown path that led to Dun Beag. Suddenly, the heavy door of the broch swung open, and a young man stepped out, a sword in his hands. His clothing was covered in dirt and blood and his eyes were wild. "Leave immediately if you value your life."

The hard metallic snap of firearms being cocked sounded behind him and Keiran turned to see two men had stepped from the treeline towards the broch. For a terrifying moment, violence thickened the air.

"I am no threat to you." Keiran stopped, splaying his hands at his sides in a gesture of surrender. "I am here to meet the Nicolsons."

"And you are?" asked a voice behind him.

"Keiran MacLeod from Clan MacLeod. My brother Alastair sent me."

The sword in the young man's hand lowered. "Apologies. We needed to be certain. We are still gathering our wits. The English set upon us only an hour ago as we waited for you to join us."

Keiran looked behind him. The rifles lowered. One older man handed his rifle to the other red-headed man before reaching inside his sporran for a folded and sealed missive that he held out to Keiran. "Take this and protect it with your life. If the English find you with a map of their whereabouts, they will show you no mercy," the elder Nicolson said.

Keiran accepted the missive and tucked it into the tail of his tartan, close to his heart. He must return with the news, and quickly, especially if the English were roaming the area. "Thank you for the information. I will make certain Alastair sees it before nightfall."

The elder Nicholson offered a nod. "Safe journey, MacLeod."

Keiran returned to his horse and set off at a swift trot back up the hilly terrain. He would find a safer place well away from Struan to allow his horse a rest. For now, they had to journey on and keep the information he'd gathered from the Nicolsons safe.

After a brisk hour of riding, Keiran slowed his horse to a stop near a creek that was just deep enough for horse and man to refresh themselves. The afternoon sunshine filtered through the trees, lending a quiet peacefulness to the area. For a moment, Keiran allowed himself to relax near the creek, reclining on a bed of tall grass. He closed his eyes and listened to the gentle rustling of the wind as it moved through the tender blades.

He wasn't certain how much time had passed when the whispering of the wind shifted to a soft thumping, then a sharper thudding. He sat upright just as a horse shrieked in the distance, followed by the clanging of steel against steel.

Keiran's heart pounded wildly as he saw ten men dressed in bright red coats surge towards another contingent of five men dressed in drab travel clothes. A heartbeat later, Keiran saw a splash of green silk, a length of brown hair, and a slim figure among the drably dressed men.

A woman. His breath caught as the men in red set upon the entire travelling party, savagely slicing anyone in their path.

A feminine cry pierced the air.

Abandoning sanity and self-preservation, Keiran mounted his horse and drew his sword. He shifted his weight forward. His horse understood the command. Together they charged through a sea of red towards that strangely misplaced femineity floating on a sea of death.

His mission had been to stay in the shadows, but how could he when a woman's life was at stake?

CHAPTER TWO

THE WOMAN RODE through the madness, avoiding swords, men, and horses. As Keiran came ever closer, he could see a thin, graceful form, a riot of shining brown hair, and wide frightened eyes.

The clash of steel and the cries of men echoed all around him. Keiran tried to block out the sound as he focused on the woman in the distance. She held no weapon. Instead, she kicked out her booted feet at a soldier who had ventured too close to her horse. The kick worked temporarily, until the man came around from the back, avoiding her feet.

Keiran leaned forward, pushing his horse to greater speed. Men in red coats fell before him, but before he could reach the woman, the soldier did. He raised his sword, turned it, brought it down.

"Stop!" Keiran cried out. The soldier's hand hesitated, but only for a second. Not long enough. He stabbed the woman, piercing her body. Keiran was too late. She tumbled to the ground like a puppet whose strings had been cut.

Keiran slashed his way past two more soldiers as his gaze connected with her pain-filled hazel eyes, before the tension in her face eased and her eyes drifted closed.

"Nay!" Keiran's cry echoed in the afternoon air. At the sight of him, the stabbing man and another of the redcoats turned their horses to the south and raced away. All the other men, her escorts and the red coats, had fallen to the ground and were dead or dying.

Keiran dismounted and raced to her side, falling to his knees beside her. She lay with one hand covering the wound in her stomach. Blood stained her long delicate fingers. Keiran placed his hand over hers and pressed down hard, trying to stem the flow of blood, to no avail. It seeped through his fingers rapidly draining from her body.

He felt the pain of her wound inside himself. Such a thing had happened before with animals who were killed in Fairyland, but never a fairy. Yet now he felt the pain and anguish of this human female. Forcing his own pain aside, with his free hand he gently brushed the hair away from her face; her skin was growing ashen, the blush of life drawing quickly away. Her eyelids fluttered open at his touch. Her eyes were no longer filled with pain, but serene. Her lips moved yet uttered no sound.

"Do not give up," he said urgently. "You must fight. I'll get you help."

She raised her hand to cover his near her face. Her fingers were cold. "Kindness in the end. Thank you." Her voice was a mere whisper of sound. A little smile moved to her lips as her hand tightened around his. Then her eyelids closed again, and the hand dropped. She lay still.

A cry began down in the pit of his stomach. When it emerged, it was as wild and untamed as the hills around him. The sound poured from Keiran's throat as pain knotted his chest. He did not know this woman, and yet he felt a connection deep within his soul. Her chest rose as though she drew one last breath.

⁓

As PAIN OVERWHELMED her senses, Rosalyn watched the man before her fade farther into the distance and a chill settled into her body. A part of her essence left her body to hover above it, floating as she watched the man drop her hand, drawing a sword, dispatching one of the English soldiers who challenged him.

"Why are you defending her?" Another soldier charged. "Her blood is not pure. She is not English or Scottish like you or me. She is an abomination."

This was no unfortunate attack. Someone had planned to kill her here in the woods.

"You killed her," said the man who had raced to her side.

"The world is better off without her," the soldier said.

The words could no longer hurt her as she had no body to process the pain. Who had sent these soldiers to kill her? Had her grandparents sent a regiment to Scotland to finally snuff out the taint they perceived her to be? She looked down on her body, saw the blood flow from her wound and saw her face turn grey.

The man with soulful eyes struck down the soldier and hurried back to her side, pulling her head into his lap. There was an odd sort of light around him that was not of this world. It was bright, shimmering, and comprised of all the colours she had seen in a rainbow.

As he brought his hands to her chest, what had once floated above, dove back inside her shell as if she were diving into a pool of darkness and did not know how to swim. Panic flared, as she instinctively reached out, trying to claw her way back to the surface, gasping for air that was no longer there.

And when she could not take that breath, when the world around her dissolved into swirling tendrils of darkness, she surrendered, and time lost its grip over her. Seconds stretched into eternity. She had no body, no weight, just pure consciousness adrift in a velvet silence.

Memories swirled before her. Some recollections of her youth with her mother and father were vibrant, and filled with laughter, others were dark, and evoked only pain and regret.

KEIRAN CLOSED HIS eyes, gathering from nature around him the one gift the fairies had given him. His muscles tightened;

warmth gathered in his hands. He let the sensation flow through him, waiting for the right moment.

A heartbeat later, he shifted that warmth from his hands into the woman's body. He had done this same thing to a few animals since his return to Dunvegan, surprised that Oberon had not taken away his gift of healing when Keiran had left Fairyland. Perhaps the fairy king did not see such an ability as important. Keiran had been given the power to heal only because of his own frail nature when compared to the other fairies. Could he use those healing powers to bring a human back from the edge of death? He had never tried before.

Keiran felt the warmth leave his hands and enter her body. A tinge of pink reanimated her face, but her chest remained still. Closing his eyes, he concentrated on the heat leaving him and flowing into her until finally her chest rose beneath his hands.

ROSALYN SAW A flicker. A spark in the distance, faint but insistent, pulled at her with the promise of air and warmth. Her will to survive flared as she reached, not with limb but with her essence towards that growing light.

Suddenly, the same rainbow colours crashed over her, primal and magnificent. Sensation once again flooded her body and just as quickly, pain flared, sharp and hot, only to slowly fade away.

KEIRAN OPENED HIS eyes as the world swam, swirled around him. He drew a deep breath, trying to replenish the energy he had given her. The animals he healed never strained his energy, but he had experienced this same sensation when he had healed himself after a fall that snapped the bone in his arm.

When his vision cleared, he looked out at the fallen men around her. Their bodies were limp and twisted. When he regained his strength, he would try to help those who still lived.

His gaze returned to her face. Her eyes were still closed, but tears spilled from beneath her dark lashes to race past a small, straight nose and onto chiselled cheekbones. Yet what fascinated him most of all was the smattering of freckles across her alabaster skin. Instead of detracting from her beauty, the small reddish marks only heightened her appeal.

Keiran studied the spots. There was a small cluster on her left cheek that almost looked as though the freckles were smiling at him. His gaze dropped to her mouth, and he swallowed hard. He was so close. Close enough to kiss her. A kiss was not part of the healing, but he could justify that it was, as all logic fled from his mind. "I promise to keep you safe," he whispered, closing the distance between them and gently brushing his lips against hers. He should have felt the softness of her flesh. Instead, a pulse of magic flared, moving back from her into him, sending tingles across his flesh. How was such a thing possible?

The woman in his arms inhaled sharply and her eyes drifted open. Deep hazel pools of colour stared up at him. Her tongue came out to moisten her lips. She tried to speak, but only a small sound came forth. She swallowed roughly and tried again. "Who . . . who are you?"

"Lie still. You were injured. Give your body time to heal." He drew back slightly, still pondering how she had been able to pass a bit of his magic back to him.

She tensed. "Do not . . . leave me."

"I am not going anywhere," he whispered, leaning into her once more. At the close contact, her eyes drifted closed, and Keiran could feel the heat he had put there, heat that would eventually completely heal her wound.

Keiran studied her face as a tinge of pink returned to her cheeks. This woman, whoever she was, unsettled him. And he was usually not unsettled by anything. From the moment he'd first seen her among her men, he'd been assailed by unfamiliar emotions, half of which he could neither name nor identify. Part of him wanted to kiss her again to see if that flare of magic would return, another part of him wanted to run as far and as fast away from her as he could.

And yet, he simply held her as the afternoon sun drifted lower towards the horizon. After she relaxed and appeared as if she were asleep, he lifted her in his arms and moved her out of the pool of blood in which they sat, onto fresh spring grass. He had just settled her into the grass when her eyes fluttered open.

"Was it a dream?" she asked, looking up at him. Her hands drifted to her midriff, exploring the wet, sticky blood his magic could not remove. With a furrowed brow, she lifted bloody hands from her stomach and brought them before her eyes.

She flinched. "I was dying. I remember seeing the world slipping away." Her forehead creased. "Then there was you. I saw you fighting the British soldiers." She tried to sit up. "British soldiers? Why were they attacking me?"

Keiran supported her back until she could sit up on her own. It was then that Keiran saw more clearly the deep bruise upon her cheek, the cut to her lip, and that one eye was starting to discolour. "Why is it so surprising that the British attacked you?"

"Because I am English." Her breath came in big gulps, and trembling shook her body. "My own people attacked me." Then her eyes widened. "One of them called me an abomination."

"Shh," he said in a soothing tone. "It is all right. You are safe with me." Keiran tightened his arm about her waist.

She glanced about her at the bodies on the ground and tears welled in her eyes. "Matthew, Henry, Richard, Thomas, and Fredrick . . . they are . . . all dead. Why? Who would hate me this much?" The woman's voice shook with pain and shock, making it difficult to understand her words. She took a deep breath and ran a hand across her face, wincing at the pain of her own touch as she tried to collect herself.

"The English soldiers came out of nowhere," she continued. "I tried to move away, out of the conflict, but he kept pursuing me. He lifted his sword . . . I tried to make him stop . . . but he stabbed me." Her hands returned to her blood-soaked dress. Her fingers poked through the hole in her once lovely gown. A sob tore from her throat, and she turned her face into Keiran's chest. He let her cry until the worst of her tears were past.

Worried about the passing of time and the possibility of more Englishmen in the vicinity, Keiran finally said in his calmest voice, "Come, we should check for survivors and get you to a safer location."

At her nod, Keiran stood, taking the woman with him. She was quiet now as she wiped the tears from her cheeks with her arm. Carefully, Keiran lifted her into his arms and set her on the back of her horse.

"Thank you for staying nearby, Petunia," she cooed to the brown and white mare. The dutiful animal had stayed near her mistress all through the fighting and had lingered even when the woman had been injured.

Keiran moved to each of the men nearby.

"Do any of my men yet live?" she asked hopefully.

He shook his head and turned away from the crestfallen

look that tugged at his heart. He moved to the redcoats. Eight remained and, of those, only one man still breathed, though barely. Not wanting to demonstrate his healing powers in front of the woman, Keiran lifted the man and placed him in front of the saddle across his horse, face down. Then he mounted behind the fallen soldier. "Come, we will find safety back at Dunvegan."

"I have heard of that castle before. It is home to the MacLeods." Her gaze shifted from his face to his tartan then back again, her eyes wide with fear. "You are a Scot?"

"I am the man who saved you. What does my being Scottish have to do with anything?" he asked, confused by her response.

The fear lessened in her eyes. "You do not look to be one of the barbarians my brother always made the Scots out to be."

"And you do not look to be the monster my brothers claim the English are." He looked back at the red-coated men on the ground. "Though these men might prove my brothers correct. You have no idea why they were attacking you?"

She sobered and shook her head. "Nothing that makes sense."

He mounted his horse behind the last living redcoat. "Perhaps this man might be able to shed some light on that situation when we take him back to Dunvegan." Shifting his attention from the man to the woman on the horse beside him, he asked, "Are you able to ride or should I lead your horse?" The horses tossed their heads as though eager to be underway and away from the battlefield.

Her brows came together as she stared down at the hole in her dress. He almost thought she did not hear him when she brought her gaze back to his. "I still do not understand what has happened to me, but I believe I am capable of riding."

With a nod, he set his horse in motion. Hers followed beside him. "Since we are to be acquainted for a while until we figure out how to send you safely home, might I know your name?"

"You'll send me home?" she asked, her eyes wide with surprise.

"Of course. The MacLeods have no need of an English prisoner when the country is swarming with English soldiers."

"If you know where the soldiers are, you could leave me with one of the regiments."

He raised a brow. "And cause a repeat of what has just happened? I do not think that is wise."

She hesitated then nodded. "You are probably correct. With you carrying one of their men, and until we know why I was attacked, it is best to stay away." She frowned. "But how will we avoid the soldiers if they are everywhere?"

Keiran hesitated for a moment, wondering if he should reveal such important information. With no other option available to him, he said, "I have a map of where the English regiments are located."

She scowled. "Then perhaps you should take it out and read it so that we might travel in relative safety."

He looked away. "If only I could."

"What does that mean?" Her irritation turned to curiosity.

He turned back to her with the realisation he had yet to admit his failings to anyone at Dunvegan. Why would he consider doing so to a stranger he did not yet trust? Then again, he had revealed his secret mission to her. "I cannot read. I was never taught how."

A startled expression crossed her face before she masked it. "Did your parents never teach you?"

"My mother died shortly after I was born, and my father—well, he was not a teacher."

"Did the MacLeods not have a tutor then?"

"I am certain my brothers did."

A frown settled between her brows. "Yet no one in your family taught you?"

"'Tis complicated," he replied, suddenly wishing he'd never told her.

"I'll teach you," she said with a warmth in her voice, then started as if surprised she had made such an offer. "My name is Rosalyn," she said abruptly, as though wishing to change the subject. "Rosalyn de Clare."

Her smile brought back the warmth he'd experienced

earlier at sunrise. "Keiran MacLeod."

"Would you like me to read the map for you, Keiran?"

Could he trust her? She was English after all, and his brothers had been very clear that the English were not honourable as a people. But could one lone Englishwoman be dependable in a life-or-death situation? Perhaps he would test her first. "Do you know where we are now?"

"My men—" Her throat caught on the word. She looked numb and achingly fragile. "My men said we were just south of Struan."

"Where were you going, Rosalyn—for you are a long way from England?"

"Only because you saved my life am I trusting you." Rosalyn dropped her gaze to the reins in her hand. "I was on my way to join my betrothed. He wished to marry me while still in service to the fifty-fifth regiment as its lieutenant."

"You were to marry an English soldier and yet you were set upon by other English soldiers?" Keiran frowned down at the body before him. "We had best return to Dunvegan before this man dies. I am certain he has an explanation that I would very much like to hear."

She reined her horse to a stop. "As would I," she echoed, and held out her hand.

Keiran reached into the folds of his tartan and produced the missive. He brought his horse alongside hers, ready to grab the reins if she decided to bolt with the information he'd been sent to gather. Carefully, she broke the seal and unfolded the message while Keiran leaned over to see the contents. There were no pictures on the page, only handwriting that he would have to trust her to interpret.

"There are three regiments in very close proximity to us." Her gaze darted into the distance and her body tensed. "One belongs to my betrothed, James Long."

Keiran reached for the missive with one hand, and her reins with the other. "Do not be a fool, thinking you can ride to him for assistance. Or have you forgotten that one of the regiments, and quite possibly his, sent men here to kill you and your men?"

"James would never," she said with hesitation in her voice. She reached for her reins, but he pulled them out of her grasp.

"Would you risk your life on that assumption? Because I will not." He kicked his horse into a gallop, forcing hers to follow. If the two men who had escaped the fray earlier knew where to find the other regiments, then he and Rosalyn had best leave this area, and quickly, before those men could return with reinforcements. "Do not even consider jumping to the ground. At this speed you will be seriously injured."

She threw him a mutinous glance as she clutched the saddle. "You are a barbarian after all."

"And you are an ungrateful shrew."

She looked away, obviously hurt by his words. But he didn't take them back. Her avoidance would give him a chance to heal the soldier on the saddle before him, because only he could give them the answers they needed.

As quickly as he could, Keiran healed the man but stopped short of a full healing so the Englishman would not cause any trouble as they made their way to Dunvegan.

Rosalyn still did not look at him. Instead, she focused on the scenery. But Keiran noticed her. Since she was riding astride, her bloodstained skirt fell untidily over her knees and the motion of the horses lifted the hem of her skirt to reveal trim and shapely ankles. When a surge of warmth pooled in his loins, he too gazed with rapt attention at the path ahead.

All that mattered at this moment was keeping a clear head and leaving this place of violence and death, though he doubted either he or Rosalyn would ever forget what had happened here.

CHAPTER THREE

ROSALYN CLUNG TO her saddle, heart pounding at the rapid pace Keiran had set. The Scottish hillsides passed before her in a blur of green and gold. His haste made it evident he wanted to avoid the English soldiers. Did she want to avoid them as well? She wasn't certain what she wanted anymore.

The morning had started with such a clear purpose. She was to be married by the end of the day, regardless of her opinion on the matter. Hugh had given her no choice. She was either to marry Lieutenant James Long after travelling to his regiment in Scotland, or she would be abandoned, ostracised by her family and society.

Without listening to her pleas about what had happened between herself and Lieutenant Long, Hugh had sent her to Scotland two days later, escorted by his finest men. And now those brave lads were all dead. Rosalyn's chest tightened at the memory of their broken and bloody bodies. Her brother would lay their deaths at her feet, of that she was certain.

Yet she'd survived. Why? She remembered feeling the blade as it penetrated her body, and the bloody warmth that followed. She had fallen to the ground, and she remembered seeing Keiran racing towards her. As a chill had numbed her limbs, and her senses had faded, she thought she remembered being pulled into a warm embrace. Then warmth had flared and something as light as a feather had brushed against her lips. A kiss? Nay, it couldn't be. The one she had shared with James had been rough and intense. Not a gentle caress as sweet as a summer's breeze.

It must be only her imagination, as was the blade that had pierced her body. Her fear must have been so intense it conjured the vivid impression from thin air. And yet... releasing her hold on the saddle with one hand, her fingers probed the bloody hole in her dress. She frowned. If she had not been assaulted, then what had caused the damage to her gown and the blood surrounding the area? It made no sense.

Her gaze lifted to the man pulling her horse alongside his. His features were set in deep concentration as he scanned the area they raced through, searching for possible danger. Had Keiran somehow erased the damage to her body? Could such a thing be possible? Perhaps once they stopped their bone-jarring race across the landscape, she would demand that he tell her the truth. If a Scot was capable of such a thing.

There were so many questions she needed answered before she could determine her next course of action. Even though her captor had expected her to jump from her horse, she knew better. Where was she to go in a place that was as foreign to her as its barbaric people? A woman alone in the wilderness with no way to defend herself would not live very long. And if she were captured by anyone else, they might not be as tolerant as the man who had already apprehended her. The only choice she had was to cling to the saddle and trust he would lead her to safety as they passed through the rolling green valleys that skirted the sea.

One part of her rebelled at his seizing the reins of her horse. The other part understood it as part of an unspoken pact between them. He had trusted her with vital information, and she could use what he had shown her against him and his people. Yet she wouldn't do that, would she? How had he known?

Since the death of their parents seven years ago, Rosalyn had lived by her brother's whim and command. But only a few days ago in the park, she had ignored her better judgement and, as a result, her life was forever changed. Her defiance of society's rules and Lieutenant Long's ungentlemanly behaviour would haunt her for the rest of her life.

With a quick glance at Keiran, Rosalyn wondered if she could escape her present situation. Instead, she tightened her grip on the saddle. She knew what she could expect from her brother. He would blame her for today's tragedy. And he was not a forgiving man. But the man beside her was still a mystery. She prayed to the heavens that Keiran was God's gift rather than a curse.

Steeling herself, she turned her attention from the man

beside her and to her horse instead. Petunia's steady gait matched her own heartbeat. High overhead, a flock of gulls circled. She heard the flap of their wings, a whoosh of air, an occasional high-pitched crying call. She could smell the tangy sea air and could feel the late afternoon sun as its weak rays tried to warm all that it touched.

They rode for the next hour in silence, and as the sun started to set, they came to a rise in the hillside where Keiran brought the horses to a stop. In the distance and bathed in the light of the setting sun, Rosalyn could see a majestic fortress atop a rocky outcrop overlooking the sea. "Is that Dunvegan?" Rosalyn asked.

"Aye," Keiran replied with a sense of awe that brought her gaze to his.

His eyes were dark brown, like the earth, solid and reliable. Yet she knew no such thing about him. "If you are worried about bringing an English soldier and an English-woman home, you can leave us here."

A sudden glint of humour appeared in his eyes. "You might be surprised how happy some members of my family might be to see that I brought any female home." A Scottish brogue was evident in his speech.

What had he meant by that? Trying to disguise her uneasiness, she dropped her gaze to the bloody ruin that was her gown. "They will no doubt have questions about what has happened."

"You think?" He laughed briefly. "Prepare yourself.

Though my sisters-in-law will be thrilled to greet you, the men of the castle might be more suspicious of your presence. During a recent attack by the English, four of our men were injured. One of them can no longer walk without the aid of a cane."

Her chest tightened at the sudden realisation that she was the enemy here, not Keiran or his family. "Perhaps you should leave me here to make my own way. I do not wish to make trouble for the MacLeods." She shifted her gaze to his and saw not anger but sympathy written there.

"The wilds of the isle can be dangerous. They are no place for a woman alone. My sister-in-law, Isolde, is proof of that." He leaned over and brought his hand down to cover hers where it still rested on the saddle. Warmth flared across her fingers at the contact. "Do not fear. I will make certain you are safe here. No one will throw you in the dungeon or harm you in any way. I promise."

She met his gaze. "I have no choice but to trust you."

He withdrew his hand and shifted his gaze to the distance as though considering her words. "We have no choice but to trust each other. If you contact your family, it could bring much danger to the MacLeods."

Instead of glancing at Keiran, at the big broad chest displayed before her eyes, Rosalyn looked beyond him to the rolling hills. They had managed to escape the English patrols for now, but when the men who had escaped the conflict found other soldiers, would they start looking for the man who had saved her, or would they come here to finish what they had started in the woods? Rosalyn closed her eyes and shook her head, trying to clear her thoughts and settle her emotions. Confusion mixed with gratitude in the aftermath of the attack on her life and of being caught up by unknown forces that were out of her control. "Thank you," Rosalyn said after a time, realising that even in her confusion she could be kind.

"For what?"

"I am sorry I called you a barbarian. I want to thank you for saving my life."

He inclined his head to acknowledge her words. "I apologise as well. You are not a shrew. That was my anger speaking."

The moment was so unexpected that she drew in a ragged breath. In a matter of hours, they had gone from sniping at each other to a kind of kinship. But was it an accord that could last between two people who should be enemies?

They rode on in silence, and as they did, Rosalyn studied the castle built on an elevated rock that projected into the loch below. The cliffs surrounding the castle were steep and rugged, offering a wide view of the loch and the sea beyond. It was truly a breathtaking sight, but it did not pull her gaze as did the man beside her.

She could tell by his torso, broad shoulders, and well-muscled arms that he was a warrior. Her gaze moved back to his face, to the brown of his eyes—eyes that spoke of some deep pain as well as kindness and intelligence. His hair was dark and cropped short enough to keep it from curling, setting off his high cheekbones and strong nose. His was a compelling face, yet fiercely masculine. It was the kind of face a woman could not help staring at with interest and desire.

A fist tightened around her heart. Desire was the last thing she wanted in her life. Had her parents' experiences not warned her of its dangers? They'd both died because of their desire: her mother, because she had desired a man whose family scorned her bloodline. The de Clares had claimed Rosalyn's mother was tainted by her Scottish heritage, and after the birth of two children, they wanted no more. And although Rosalyn could never prove it, she was certain they had orchestrated the carriage accident, causing her mother's untimely death. Her father, because of his desire for her mother, at her loss he had withered away, leaving her barely-of-age brother as her guardian.

A chill ran across Rosalyn's nape. Was that what had happened in the forest near Struan? Had her father's family come after her, trying to stop her from continuing the de Clare line with her husband?

Rosalyn's gaze shifted to the man lying face down across Keiran's horse. "Do you think the English soldier will survive?" she asked, breaking the silence that had fallen between them.

"He will live to tell us why he and the others attacked

you," Keiran assured her as they approached the castle's gate. The torches had been lit and Rosalyn could see men gathered just beyond the gate on horseback. At the sight of them, a call went out to the gatekeeper and the iron portcullis rose.

As she and Keiran moved closer to those gathered, Rosalyn swallowed nervously as she clearly saw twenty Scottish men on horseback.

"Praise the heavens you have returned," exclaimed one of the men near the front of those assembled. He dismounted quickly and came towards them. "We were about to come looking for you. We had feared the worst when you did not return as expected."

Keiran slid from his horse. "The English attacked the Nicolson clan before I arrived." He withdrew the missive from the folds of his tartan and handed it to the man.

Two other men who looked very similar to the first dismounted and came forward. "Thank goodness you are still alive. I never would have forgiven myself if something had happened to you." The other similar-looking man frowned as his gaze shifted between Keiran, the soldier upon Keiran's horse, then to her and her bloodied gown. "Although it is obvious something happened."

"I was returning to Dunvegan when I came upon a skirmish in the woods. This woman's party was attacked by an English patrol. All her men were killed, and she was injured. Two of the English soldiers escaped, leaving their dead behind."

"Was injured?" one of the men asked, frowning at the blood on her dress.

"I managed to stop the worst of the bleeding, but our healer should examine her to be certain." Keiran reached up and lifted her down from her horse, keeping his hands at her waist. When he was certain she could stand on her own, Keiran stepped back and waved two of the men forward to help him with the English soldier. "This man can tell us why Rosalyn's travelling party was attacked. Take him to Lottie first to assure he lives but tie him to the bed. We cannot have him escape and inform the English where this young woman ended up."

One of the men came to stand before her. "Rosalyn?"

She nodded, shifting uncomfortably, uneasy with his scrutiny. She was the one who usually studied people. It was disconcerting for him to look at her and see . . . what? What did he see? Because he did not look at her with the same cool calculation most of the English aristocracy did.

"Welcome to Dunvegan. I am Alastair MacLeod, and these are my brothers Tormod and Orrick. Let's get you inside to a bedchamber so that Lottie, our healer, can mend your wounds. I will have my wife, Gwendolyn, supply you with clothing."

This was not what she'd expected from the Scottish people who had always been the villains in the stories told by her brother since she was young. Perhaps they were only being kind so that she would let down her guard. And for what?

She had no information about the English in the area beyond what Alastair now knew after reading Keiran's missive.

Why were they being so kind to her? She was positive the English would not be so hospitable if their situations were reversed. Even so, Rosalyn swallowed roughly as she allowed the man to lead her forward, towards a fair-haired woman waiting at the castle doorway.

"All will be well," Keiran called as she moved towards the doorway.

She glanced back at him, almost believing him. Sweet heavens, she needed someone who she could trust in this world suddenly turned upside down. Separated from her home and life in England, she was now alone in a country, surrounded by people she feared. She needed someone she could trust, someone to talk to, someone who would understand how tired she was of never being able to pursue her own dreams and goals.

Rosalyn shook herself as a gust of cold wind blew through the courtyard. What was she thinking? After the turmoil she'd been through in the past few days, had she learned nothing? Her dreams did not matter, and she could trust no one. Not her brother. Not Keiran. Her features hardened.

Keiran frowned as he turned back to speak to Tormod and Orrick.

She returned her gaze to the beautiful woman in the

doorway. At her welcoming smile something blossomed in Rosalyn's chest, but with her next heartbeat, she forced the emotion aside. These people were the enemy.

She could not stay at Dunvegan, and she could not go back to her home in London without a husband. With few other options, she would have to find a way to escape the MacLeods and make her way back to where James's regiment was located. Marriage was the only thing that would save her from ruin. Rosalyn straightened as Alastair stopped before his wife.

"Gwendolyn, meet Rosalyn. She will be staying with us for a while."

"My goodness," Gwendolyn said looking down at Rosalyn's dress. "It appears you have had a very difficult day." She reached for Rosalyn's arm, taking it gently and encouraging her forward. "Come with me. Let's get you cleaned up."

"Thank you," Rosalyn replied with a sudden tightness in her chest as she stepped inside the castle. They moved together up one staircase, then another before heading down a long hallway. As they walked, Rosalyn reminded herself that she could accept the MacLeods' kindness now, then wait for an opportunity to leave without anyone noticing.

Her future depended on it.

CHAPTER FOUR

ROSALYN DISAPPEARED FROM his view, but his thoughts continued to centre on her. He had done all he could for Rosalyn until they knew more about why she had been attacked. But if her own people had run her through with a sword, her future in England did not look promising.

The thought of her in despair, as she had been in the woods, pained him. He knew nothing about Rosalyn except that she had been abandoned by her people and was now alone in this world. He knew that feeling well. Even though he'd been under a spell during his time with the fairies, he had always known he did not belong.

Keiran wiped his forehead, feeling the grit of the dust that had settled on his skin. He clenched his jaw, suppressing the urge to go after her and assure himself she was well. He had healed her abdomen, but had he missed some other injury that could put her in danger? He balled his fists, resisting the urge. God's blood. What was wrong with him? She was betrothed to another. Even so, he'd never had this kind of reaction, this connection, to anyone before.

He stared off into the darkness as the men around him

dismounted and turned their horses over to the stable hands. He took a deep breath and unfurled his fingers. He had to stay focused on the threat to the MacLeods and all the clans on the isle. The English soldiers had shown Rosalyn's travelling party no mercy. He doubted they would be any less harsh with the Scots.

"Come," Tormod said, breaking into his thoughts. "Alastair wishes us to join him in the great hall. No doubt to discuss our response to the information you brought home."

Orrick appeared on the other side of Keiran and frowned. "Are you certain you are unharmed? You are much changed from when you left this morning."

Tormod smiled. "Forgive me for saying it, but you appear less . . . lost."

Keiran scowled at his older brothers. "The woman was in trouble. What else was I to do? Leave her to die?"

Tormod chuckled and clapped Keiran on the shoulder. "All I said was that your countenance had changed. I said nothing about the girl."

"Do not pay him heed, Keiran," Orrick said. "Of course, you are changed. You have been through an ordeal. I was simply asking if you had taken any blows we should be aware of."

"I am more concerned about the English attacking the MacLeods than I am my own physical state," Keiran replied.

"The walls of Dunvegan will protect us," Orrick assured him as they made their way inside the castle and up the stairs.

"They haven't always," Tormod reminded his brother as they moved down the hallway and to the great hall. "We must be prepared for anything."

Graeme, the captain of the guard, and Callum, their youngest brother, had joined Alastair at a table. Alastair spread out the parchment Keiran had brought before him, studying it silently. The pause gave Keiran a chance to study Callum as he sat across the table from the young man.

As if sensing Keiran's exploration, Callum lifted his eyes—eyes filled with wisdom and sorrow—before shifting his attention back to Alastair. Not for the first time did Keiran wonder what had happened to the young man in the last nine years. Had he had the childhood that Keiran had missed? Or, even here in the human realm, had Callum been forced to grow up quickly in the absence of their mother and father?

Keiran was stopped from further ruminations as Alastair passed the missive to Tormod. "It appears several English regiments have moved north. I'm anticipating more will follow in the days ahead."

"That cannot be good for the clans," Orrick said.

Alastair nodded grimly. "I have heard rumours, and the English must have as well, that with war raging across the continent, the French are open to supplying James Stuart and his son, Charles, with financing, soldiers, and ships for another advance into Scotland."

"The English must believe those rumours to be true," Graeme noted with a deep frown.

Alastair's gaze shifted to Keiran. "It was a risk, meeting up with the Nicolsons, but the reports they passed on are too important to trust to regular couriers. I'm concerned that the English army knows too much information about the Scottish clans and our business. We are going to have to try to stay ahead of their flow of information by obtaining our own, and trying to cut off whatever and whoever is supplying them with theirs."

"I would go back to Struan if you need me to do so," Keiran offered. It would be best for him to go, and alone, for if he was set upon, at least he could heal himself, keeping the rest of the MacLeods safe.

Tormod leaned his arms on the table and gazed intensely at Keiran. "Tell us what happened outside of Struan? The woman you brought home should have been dead, judging by the amount of blood on her clothing. How is she still alive?"

Keiran had expected such a question. "It was not her blood, but that of her assailant after I ran him through with my sword," he lied, holding Tormod's gaze and forcing away the remorse he felt at doing so.

To Alastair, Tormod asked, "What do you think ought to be done with the woman?"

"She stays here," Keiran interrupted. "We need to discover why she was attacked when she was on her way to meet her betrothed."

Tormod's brows rose. "And by English soldiers. Do you not find that curious?"

"Of course, I am curious as to why. Only once we have answers from the man I captured can we know how to proceed with the woman."

Tormod frowned. "If she was to meet her betrothed, she will be missed. Someone will no doubt come looking for her."

"I suspect so," Keiran agreed. "We must stay ahead of the English." He pushed his chair back and stood. "Shall we go abovestairs and question the surviving soldier?"

Tormod stood. "Aye. What will you do with the soldier after he tells you what you need to know?"

"As long as he remains useful, we should keep him here at Dunvegan," Keiran replied.

Orrick pushed back his chair but did not rise. "After that, Isolde and I can take him to Dunshee Castle and reunite him with his brethren there."

"You have English prisoners at Dunshee?" Keiran frowned. He still had so much to learn about his family and their secrets.

Orrick nodded. "We have detained what remains of a regiment that attacked Dunvegan several months ago. They are treated fairly and are not confined to the dungeon as the English would have done to us if we were captured."

An uneasy feeling settled in Keiran's gut. "Do the English know about their location?"

"No one but those of us in this chamber know that secret," Orrick replied. "The English most likely assumed they died along with the others at *Caisteal an Bháis*."

"Rosalyn can never learn about this," Keiran said in a grim tone. "Or we will all be in far more danger than we are now."

Tormod's gaze narrowed. "She is our enemy."

"We do not know that for certain, but we should be cautious until we know more about her." Keiran was suddenly eager to do just that, to learn more about the woman he had brought back to his home, to his family. If anything happened to them because of a softness he allowed himself to feel for this woman, he would never forgive himself.

"What do you think we will discover? That she is a spy?" Tormod asked.

Keiran headed for the stairs with Tormod following close behind. "I am almost positive she was merely at the wrong place at the wrong time."

"With a company of men?"

Keiran blew out a breath. "We will not know for certain until we talk to the English soldier." Determined to know why Rosalyn had been attacked and hoping she was an innocent in all of this, Keiran took the stairs two at a time, marvelling he could do so. He'd never felt the need for haste in Fairyland. With the same efficiency, he moved down the hallway until he stood outside their prisoner's chamber door.

The portal was open, and Lottie had just finished winding a bandage about the man's head where he had been nicked by a blade. Keiran stepped inside, startling the woman and the two guards who had been placed inside the chamber.

"I have completed my examination," the healer said, returning her gaze to her patient.

"Your verdict as to his health?" Keiran studied the Englishman whose arms were tied to the bedposts. His angry glare cut through the distance between them.

"He is very fortunate. There is a fresh scar on his upper thigh that should have left him unable to walk. It appears mostly healed, and there is another puncture through his ribs, as well as a wound into his liver that should have killed him. Yet he is still alive, and his wounds are . . ." The colour drained from her face. "'Tis as if his wounds are healing themselves."

Keiran nodded and moved past the healer towards the bed. "Would you please find and check on Rosalyn now?"

The healer gathered her bag of herbs and poultices and left the chamber.

"You did not seem surprised by Lottie's assessment," Tormod commented as he came around the opposite side of the bed where their prisoner lay.

Keiran ignored the comment and instead focused his attention on the man tied to the bed. He arranged his features not with anger, but with determination and strength as Oberon had taught him. In a stern voice he said, "You will tell us what we want to know, or this will not end well for you."

The soldier turned his head away from Keiran, but at the sight of Tormod's angry glare, he shifted back to Keiran. "I have nothing to say."

"Why did you and your men attack Rosalyn de Clare's travelling party?" Keiran kept his voice calm though he was anything but inside. He wanted answers now.

The man pressed his lips together and stared into the distance.

A tic started in Keiran's jaw. They did not have time to wait for the man to be compliant. As Tormod mentioned earlier, there could be an angry bridegroom out there hunting for Rosalyn. "I'll have answers from you one way or another."

The man closed his eyes.

"Looks like we'll have to torture him for answers," Tormod said, his voice filled with regret.

"Nay. Not in the traditional way at least. Guards, Tormod, would you leave us alone for a few moments?"

The guards nodded and headed out the door though Tormod remained. "I am not going anywhere."

"Very well. If you are to stay, then make yourself useful and blindfold him." Keiran held out a piece of cloth to his brother.

Tormod tied the blindfold then stepped back. "Now what?"

Having no choice but to proceed in front of his brother, Keiran brought his hand to lie on the man's chest.

At the touch from his enemy, the soldier's body stiffened. "What are you doing?"

Ignoring the prisoner and Tormod's presence, Keiran gathered a measure of heat inside himself and sent it into the man's chest like a brief bolt of lightning before pulling his hand back. He wanted to frighten the man, not kill him.

The soldier arched his back and howled in pain. When he settled against the bed once more his face was ashen, and his body trembled. "What was that?"

"Aye," Tormod asked, looking at his brother as if he was someone unknown to him. "I thought you said nay to torture."

"'Tis a little trick I learned from the fairies and is harmless," Keiran said flatly. "Tell us what we want to know, or I will be forced to do that again."

The soldier shook his head. "I'll tell you if you promise not to murder me when I do."

"Your life is safe with us. We promise." Keiran clutched his hands, fighting a wave of dizziness that came over him. He was grateful not to have to deliver another shock to receive the cooperation they needed. He still had not recovered fully from healing both Rosalyn and this man earlier. Keiran pulled the blindfold from the man's eyes.

At Tormod's nod in concurrence, the man said, "We were ordered to kill the woman and her men."

"Ordered by whom?" Keiran pressed.

The man paused and looked away from Keiran. "Lieutenant James Long."

Keiran closed his eyes for a moment. Agony rocked him as he absorbed the soldier's words. Opening them, he said in a rough whisper, "Rosalyn's betrothed ordered you to kill her?"

The man nodded.

"Have you any idea why?" Keiran asked.

"The lieutenant agreed to the betrothal under protest. He had no intention of ever marrying the girl. He only wanted to get her brother off his tail. Lieutenant Long said he would rather marry his horse than a coarse, unsophisticated woman such as Rosalyn de Clare."

Keiran knit his brow. "Why does he think her uncivilised? She is English, as is he."

The soldier swallowed roughly. "She is part Scot, therefore a part of her is unacceptable to him."

"Then he never should have agreed to marry her," Keiran exploded. "What kind of man would do something like that to be rid of a woman?"

The soldier's mouth tightened, and he shifted away from Keiran as far as his restraints would allow. "One who will come and slay your entire family without a second thought, especially now that you have taken something that once belonged to him."

"The MacLeods do not fear Lieutenant James Long or

any of the English. We can hold our own against whatever they might have in store for us. You, however, should prepare yourself to be transported on the morrow to be reunited with some of your brethren who also tried to test the MacLeods."

The soldier paled. "I am to be a prisoner?"

Keiran stood. "You wished to remain unharmed. So now you will join the others we have captured since the English invaded our lands."

"I'll stay with our prisoner until you send the guards back into the chamber," Tormod said.

Keiran stepped from the room, and signalled the guards to return, before heading down the hallway. Should he tell Rosalyn that her betrothed had tried to kill her, or was she better off not knowing? Perhaps if he saw her again, he would be better able to decide if she was a woman who wanted to know the truth or avoid it altogether.

He'd known fairies like that in Fairyland—those who had grasped the illusion of contentment and had ignored reality.

Rosalyn did not strike him as frivolous, but what did he truly know about her except that her skin was soft, her eyes were like amber glowing in the afternoon sun, and that during their brief time together, she had been the only one to break through the barrier of aloofness he had built around himself since his return.

In her presence, he had felt almost human again, a flesh-and-blood man of the earth, for the first time in nine years.

CHAPTER FIVE

"WHAT DO YOU mean she is still alive?" Lieutenant James Long released a throaty growl as anger surged through him.

"I ran her through with my sword, but then a man who was tall and burly and as savage as any man we've come across yet in this godforsaken country appeared out of nowhere, attacking us like a wild beast rising from the forest floor. He struck down two men with one swipe of his sword and another three after that. Alan and I could see our cause was lost and managed to escape before the beast came after us."

"Damn stupid louts—that's what the lot of you are." The lieutenant drew his sword and brought it to rest beneath George's chin, allowing it to cut through the delicate skin of his neck. "You should have stayed to finish him off."

"We would have died," Alan said as George swallowed roughly and took a half-step back. Blood dripped from the cut to trail down his neck. "It was inhuman the way the man fought. We thought it best to come back here and report what we saw."

"And what did you see?" the lieutenant asked, keeping his sword raised and shifting it between Alan and George's chests, trying to decide which man would pay for such incompetence. He wanted Rosalyn de Clare dead. How difficult a task was it to kill a woman? Only when she was dead would he be free of the commitment her brother had forced upon him. He had no time for marriage or women, not when his regiment was about to lead an attack on the Scots of the Isle.

"The man was travelling alone," Alan said with a quiver in his voice.

"He wore a MacLeod tartan," George added, taking yet another step back.

At their fear, a smile tugged at the corner of the lieutenant's mouth. It was about time someone saw him the way he saw himself—powerful, commanding, and superior to them all. "The MacLeods, you say." Lieutenant Long again brought his sword to Alan's chest. The man's face turned ashen. "If you two want to stay alive, then I suggest you go find out if the MacLeods have Rosalyn in their possession."

Alan nodded. "If we find her, we shall put an end to her life as you requested."

"No!" His voice was hard, filled with the power that ran through his veins. "I want her alive." The MacLeods taking what was his gave him a moral advantage he did not possess before. His cause now had a purpose: to reclaim his bride.

The lieutenant looked at the ashen faces of his men.

What were they afraid of now? "What are you waiting for? Go and find the girl then report back to me. Once we have confirmed that the MacLeods indeed possess her, we will strike, and the battle for the Highlands will begin."

In the meanwhile, he would placate the English command. They had sent orders to watch and wait only. An order he intended to disobey as soon as he knew where to strike. The MacLeods would only be the first clan to fall beneath his sword. It was time to put an end to those who were trying to bring a Stuart back to the throne.

———

ROSALYN WATCHED WITH fascination as the healer examined her abdomen. Where she could swear there had been a ragged red scar not an hour ago, only a fine sliver of pink remained.

"You are certain you were stabbed with a sword?" the healer asked with a befuddled expression.

Rosalyn pointed to the hole in her discarded dress. "The evidence lies there. Yet I am, as you say, unharmed."

Lottie straightened and shrugged. Her features cleared. "Perhaps we should stop trying to understand and just accept. You are very fortunate Keiran came upon you when he did. Too many times I have seen men after battles like the one you were in. They are never the same again."

Rosalyn nodded. She wasn't certain she would ever be

the same again either, even though she had now been spared from permanent injury. "Thank you." She managed to force the words from a throat that had suddenly gone tight. Her whole world had been turned upside down in a matter of days. Had her situation gone from bad to worse, or had she ended up in a place and with a family who were as kind as they seemed?

Rosalyn's gaze shifted to Gwendolyn who had stood quietly at the end of the bed all through Lottie's examination. When the healer departed, she came to sit beside Rosalyn on the bed. "I cannot imagine what you must be feeling right now. Attacked by your own people and whisked back to a fortress where you do not know a thing about the residents who live here." She offered up a sympathetic smile. "Would it help if I assured you that we only want to help you? That you are truly safe here?"

The odd thing was, Rosalyn did feel safe, probably safer than she had ever felt living in London after the death of her parents. Even so, she raised her head and met Gwendolyn's gaze with strength. "I am grateful to have a temporary safe harbour, but I will not be staying long."

Gwendolyn frowned. "Have you somewhere else to go?"

"I am your enemy. Why would you want me to stay?"

"It matters not which side of Hadrian's Wall you were born on. You are human and in need of a bath, a meal, and some sleep, I am certain."

"You do not care that I am English?"

"If you do not care that I am Scottish." Gwendolyn opened her hand to reveal a key. "Here, take this. You will have the only key to your chamber. I am certain it will help you to sleep better knowing no one else can enter your chamber unless you allow it."

As if disproving that very point, a soft rap sounded before the door opened and a red-haired woman stepped inside, carrying an armful of gowns and other various garments. "Good evening, Rosalyn. I am Fiona. I gathered up everything you might need," she said, setting the pile of clothing on the bed. There were three gowns, two shifts, and two night rails, stays, hose, and so much more. "Our chatelaine is still rounding up a few more items as well as shoes and a cloak. And Isolde is right behind me."

She had barely finished speaking when a tall, thin blond entered the chamber, followed by three men who carried a hip bath and several buckets of steaming water. "We brought water for a bath," Isolde said, joining the others near the bed. "Mrs Honey will be along any moment with a tray for your dinner."

As if on cue, Mrs Honey entered with a tray containing a meat pie, fruit compote, a hearty slice of cheese and bread, and a mug of ale, which she set on a table near the fire. She offered Rosalyn a smile and a quick curtsy before heading from the chamber. Taking charge of those who had entered, Gwendolyn motioned for the men to set the hip bath near the fire. They filled it with their buckets of steaming water and departed.

Reading Rosalyn's puzzled expression, Isolde replied, "We thought you might be tired and would rather eat in your chamber tonight instead of facing the entire family while you are still recovering from today's trauma."

"I do not know what to say," Rosalyn said hesitantly. "I suspected I would be thrown in the dungeon as a prisoner of the MacLeods. Why would you care about my comfort at all?"

Gwendolyn pressed the key into Rosalyn's hand. "You are not a prisoner. You are free to leave whenever you would like."

Isolde came forward. "I would caution you from departing without a definite plan or a place to go, though. The wilderness of the isle can be dangerous for a woman alone."

Rosalyn recalled Keiran saying something about Isolde living in isolation for over a year. Perhaps Rosalyn could learn some of the woman's secrets if she stayed a few days more. "I would very much like to bathe and to refresh myself. Thank you, all." She hesitated before continuing, "I did not expect such kindness."

"Let me guess," Fiona said. "You were told stories all your life about the uncivilised nature of the Scots."

Reluctantly, Rosalyn nodded.

"We heard the same stories about the English," Fiona replied with a grin. "Let us make up our own minds about each other, shall we?"

Rosalyn looked at the three women before her—Gwendolyn, Isolde, and Fiona. They did not appear threatening in any way, and if she were honest, she rather liked all three women. They were the kind of women—intelligent, interesting, and open-minded—that she had always dreamed of having as friends. She had never had women she could laugh with, or discuss the issues of the day, or anyone who cared whether she was happy. Friends who would give purpose to her life. Rosalyn swallowed hard, realising all this was happening so suddenly. "I am grateful for your assistance this evening, but as you suspected, I am exhausted. I would very much like a bath and to go to sleep."

"Will you need any assistance removing that gown?" Isolde asked.

Rosalyn shook her head. She had been without a maid for years and was used to taking care of her own needs.

"Very well," Isolde replied. "When you are ready, simply place your soiled garment outside your door and our laundress will try to remove the stains and repair it, if you'd like."

Rosalyn nodded. As the women departed, her throat tightened. This day had not started out well, had been one of the worst in her life, and yet she could honestly say it had ended far better than she ever could have imagined.

Still not wanting to put all her trust in the MacLeods until she knew them better, she moved to the door and locked herself in the chamber. Then, placing the key on the stand beside the bed, she began to remove her dress. The blood had dried, making the fabric stiff as she pulled it over her head, then tossed it to the floor.

The room was warm with the fire and relatively bright despite the deepening darkness outside the window. Rosalyn ran her fingers through her hair, working out the knots and picking pieces of grass and leaves from the mass before stepping into the tub. As she submerged herself in the steaming water, her thoughts returned to the man who had brought her to this place.

She had decided to give the women of Dunvegan a chance to be friends. Should she offer the same to Keiran? Her gaze dropped to the barely discernible scar on her abdomen. She wasn't certain what he had done to her, but he had kept her alive. No matter what tale he had spun to divert attention from himself, she knew the blood on her dress had been hers. She would never forget the feel of the sticky warmth running through her fingers and her life draining from her.

There was something about Keiran that was different from her brother, and even his own brothers and Lieutenant James Long. Keiran was as strong and commanding as any of the others, but there was another intangible element that drew her gaze more often than she cared to admit. In him, she recognised a part of herself, a part that had been so filled with loneliness there was no more space inside her for anything but pain. But how could someone, who had been raised with a family who was so welcoming and kind, be filled with such despair?

If she wanted to find out why, and to repay Keiran for saving her life, she would have to stay at Dunvegan for at least a short while. At her decision, a sense of exhilaration moved through her. For the first time in her life, she could decide her own fate. She had no idea what it was that she wanted except the freedom to make her own choices.

The fear and trepidation that had haunted her all day was forced aside by a blossoming joy. After washing her body and her hair, she stood and dried herself quickly with the bath sheet Gwendolyn had left nearby, then dressed herself in a shift and a simple rust-coloured dress with tiny gold leaves embroidered around the edges of the bodice and hem. She could have opted for a night rail as she was determined to stay in her chamber, but a dress felt like a safer choice in the house of her enemy.

Idly, Rosalyn traced the embroidery threads with her fingers. The dress was not something she would ever have dared to wear in London. It was too plain for that. But it was the dress's simplicity that she liked, that and the way it made her feel—like she didn't have to pretend to be anything but herself.

She was no longer in London. She was no longer under her brother's thumb. And she was no longer on her way to be married to a man she didn't fully know and certainly didn't love. Rosalyn drew a long shaky breath. Not that she was holding out for a love match. She feared the kind of passion that had led to her parents' deaths. Yet she had hoped to at least share a closeness, a friendship with the person who she would commit to for the rest of her life. Now that she had been spared, at least temporarily, her thoughts drifted back to Keiran and the MacLeods.

Without his knowing it, Keiran had given her back a small glimmer of hope that her life might amount to something. She had always dreamed of running her own household, being the kind of mistress who would treat her entire household with kindness, perhaps teaching the young children of their staff how to read, write, and do basic arithmetic. Their lives would be much improved as a result.

Or were those things only a dream that would go unfulfilled due to her own dire situation? The MacLeods had been very kind so far, but would they allow her to remain with them more than a few days?

With every passing moment, Rosalyn knew she did not want to resume her journey towards marrying Lieutenant James Long. She doubted he would allow her to do anything except be his wife, especially here in Scotland while he served his regiment.

Rosalyn pressed her lips together in thought. Today's experiences had made her long for so much more. Perhaps on the morrow, she could make good on her promise to teach Keiran how to read. Then she could find other children who might need her help here at Dunvegan. Once she successfully tutored Keiran and others, perhaps the Mac-

Leods would provide her with a reference so that she could venture out on her own as Hugh had never allowed her in England.

A familiar hurt centred in her chest. Damn her brother for never believing in her or allowing her to follow her own path. Rosalyn straightened. If she had learned anything by the day's events, it was that she was a survivor. She might have had help from Keiran to live through that battle, but she would not take his gift and waste it. She had been given a second chance to live her life. What she would do with it was now up to her.

CHAPTER SIX

K EIRAN WALKED PAST the drawing room after finishing his talk with the English soldier and stopped at the doorway. On the opposite wall hung the Fairy Flag, protected between plates of glass. The ancient relic called to him, and he stepped inside the chamber, going to stand before the faded yellow silk with embroidered red elf dots and crosses upon it. He had heard Oberon speak of the magical cloth in the fairy realm. But he had not realised the value it had for his clan until Aria and Graeme had come to trade the artifact for his safe return to the human realm.

They had not been forced to sacrifice the priceless treasure, as they had defeated the fairy king before he had taken possession. Yet once Oberon managed a return to Fairyland from whatever void he had been cast into by the fairies' combined forces, he would want to reclaim the magical flag his daughter, Pearl, had given to the MacLeods centuries ago.

Keiran stepped closer, examining the relic. Except this was not the original Fairy Flag. If it were, he would see a soft silver aura about it as he did when he looked at Aria with her magical white glow. Everything that came out of Fairyland had an aura. Keiran's aura was purple even though he had been born to the human realm. He was almost certain no one here at Dunvegan, except Aria and perhaps his mother, could see auras.

He reached out to touch the glass protecting the magical cloth and wondered where the real Fairy Flag had gone.

At a shuffle in the doorway, Keiran turned, his hand on his sword. At the sight of his brothers Alastair, Tormod, and Orrick, Keiran relaxed his grip.

"There you are," Alastair said, stepping into the chamber. His blue-green aura, the signs of a leader and peacemaker, warmed the chamber. "We have been looking for you." Tormod and Orrick entered behind their brother.

Keiran turned back to the flag. "Why do you have a replica of the Fairy Flag?"

"How did you know it was a copy?" Orrick came to stand beside Keiran, Orrick's yellow aura mixing with Keiran's own purple to create brown. Keiran wished he could see his family for what they were without seeing the soft colours hovering around them, but at least he knew what he could expect from each of them. Orrick was a logical, cheerful person whereas Tormod was the strong and energetic brother with his red aura.

"I can see when things are touched with magic, and this cloth is not, yet all of you are."

"You can see the hint of fairy blood that runs in our

veins?" Orrick lifted his arm and squinted his eyes, searching for the aura Keiran could easily see.

"Come, sit." Alastair took a seat in one of the four tall-backed chairs near the hearth. "There is much to discuss."

Keiran and his brothers took up the other three chairs as Alastair explained, "The real Fairy Flag has been kept hidden after the MacDonald clan tried to steal it last year. We would be happy to show you where we keep the true Fairy Flag."

"Nay. I do not want to know that secret. My not knowing will keep the treasure safe." Despite the boon they had offered him, Keiran frowned. "The flag you sent with Aria to Fairyland was the replica then?"

"The plan was to get you out of Fairyland before Oberon discovered the truth," Tormod said, crossing his long legs before him.

Despite having been returned to his birth family and thrilled to be amongst them once again, if Keiran were honest, there was still a part of him that held a fondness for the fairy king who had raised him. "Oberon would have been furious had he discovered that truth." Keiran's gaze returned to the replica of the flag. "Even though this copy can fool everyone else, it will not fool Oberon for long when he is in its presence."

"That will be difficult for him to do since he is dead," Tormod snorted. When Keiran did not join in his amusement, Tormod's features turned serious. "He is dead, is he not?"

"Nay," Keiran admitted. He realised in that moment his brothers would want to know the truth. They would want to know their enemy might return rather than live in ignorance. "It would take a lot more than a little fairy magic to turn Oberon into dust. He most likely was transported to another realm, or another time. And when he discovers how to reverse what the other fairies have done, he will return to punish those who upended his life and his reign over the fairies."

"I suspected as much." Alastair leaned forward. "I am not worried about the Fairy Flag, but how do we keep you safe? Because if Oberon comes here, he'll want to take you back with him, will he not?"

Keiran shrugged. "I do not know, but now is not the time to worry about such things. It could take Oberon years to find his way back."

"How were you able to force the soldier to talk?" Orrick suddenly interrupted. At Keiran's startled expression, Orrick continued. "I was watching from the doorway. You placed your hand on him and there was a flash of light that passed from you into the man. What was that?"

"You could see the light?" A heaviness came to Keiran's throat, and he cursed himself for it. These were his brothers, yet he was suddenly afraid of what they might think of him when they learned the truth.

Orrick's gaze continued to probe Keiran's.

He straightened and turned his head away, hiding his

sudden fear.

"Trust in us, Keiran."

He glanced back at Orrick, Tormod, then Alastair. Their faces were filled with more concern than curiosity. Sweet heavens, he wanted to trust them. After two weeks in their presence, he knew they would be understanding. He needed someone to confide in. He was so alone at times.

"I am not the brother who left here nine years ago. I am changed in many ways," Keiran admitted.

"None of us are the same," Orrick said. "Your absence and Mother and Father's deaths changed us all."

"'Tis more than that." Keiran paused and drew a fortifying breath. Better to say this quickly. His brothers knew something was different about him. They would only keep asking. It was time to tell them the truth. "Oberon did not like having an infant in his court, so within a few days of my arrival in Fairyland, he aged me to ten and four years of age. What he did not realise about humans was that in their teenage years, they are clumsy and sometimes moody.

"As I accompanied the other fairies in their activities and learned the ways of fairy life, I kept falling out of trees, tripping over roots in the forest, slashing my leg on the ragged rocks along the shoreline. I even stabbed myself as I was learning how to battle, not to mention the wounds I incurred from the blades of others.

"Frustrated by always having to mend my frail body when compared to the sturdiness of the fae folk, Oberon cast a spell, imbuing me with the powers of healing and death. He changed me, turning me into the male counterpart to the Celtic goddess Morrigan. I have not explored all the facets of magic he gifted me with, but I know I can heal, or take away life. The other fairies told me I could also manipulate the weather, the elements, and the minds of others, though I have never tried. I embody both life and death, creation and destruction, order and chaos."

When he had finished with his confession, Keiran sank back against his chair, suddenly exhausted, waiting for his brothers to say something, anything. But they simply stared at him with a mixture of awe and confusion.

"Oberon did not take those powers away from you when you left Fairyland?" Alastair asked, breaking the silence.

"I do not think he remembered he had given them to me, or I am certain he would have. The other fairies tended to avoid me. They were jealous that I was considered a favoured son even though I was human. And the only times I ever used my powers in Fairyland was to heal myself, so not many might remember I even had them."

"This is truly amazing, Keiran. With your powers we have an edge we did not possess before when fighting our enemies. Yet only you shall decide how it is to be used." Alastair's gaze was filled with awe for a moment before the look faded. "And though you were given this gift, it came at a terrible price, we now realise. You were alone for a long time, but no more." Alastair reached out and placed his hand on Keiran's arm. "You are a MacLeod, our family, our brother, and we love you."

"You never had a chance to be a child?" Orrick's gaze connected with Keiran's. "You were forced into adulthood so quickly and were given not necessarily a gift, but a huge burden with your powers."

"That explains the response the soldier had when you touched him," Tormod said. "You were draining a bit of life from him with your hands."

Keiran nodded. "It was not my intent to harm him in any lasting way. Only to get him to talk."

"The man's wounds, Rosalyn's wounds—you healed them?" Alastair asked.

Again, Keiran nodded. "I could not let Rosalyn die on that battlefield. And the soldier possessed information I needed to try to keep her safe." Keiran turned to look at Alastair. "Now that we know it was Rosalyn's betrothed who order her death, what will you do with the soldier?"

"Our plans have not changed," Orrick said. "Isolde and I will take him back to Dunshee Castle to be with the other English soldiers."

"And what will happen to Rosalyn?" Keiran asked, hoping Alastair would allow her to stay. "She still needs to heal, and it is impossible for her to continue towards her betrothed and survive."

"She can stay if she likes, Keiran. But she did not seem the kind of woman who would do well without a purpose for long," Alastair said.

Keiran knew all too well what it felt like to not have a purpose. He would help her find one. He did not have to see into the future to know that if she left, death surely awaited her, especially in the arms of Lieutenant James Long.

CHAPTER SEVEN

A T DAWN THE next morning, Rosalyn crept silently out of the castle and into the rear courtyard, moving to the crenellated wall that looked out over Loch Dunvegan. She gathered the cloak that had been left outside her locked chamber door around her shoulders as she drew a breath of the salt-laced air. The sky was painted with shades of pink, purple, orange, and blue as the sun slowly rose over the horizon. The light reflected off the water and the misty hills in the distance.

When she was in London, Rosalyn had loved this time of the morning when everyone else was still abed. She would put on a coat and head outside to watch the sun rise over the city, feeling its vitality energise her. But here at Dunvegan where the air smelled both sweet and salty, and birdsong and the waves gently lapping at the shore were the only sounds, she experienced a rebirth of spirit. The day lay before her, an open slate filled with possibility.

"What are you doing?" a male voice came at her from behind.

Rosalyn turned to face Keiran. "Haven't you ever seen

anyone enjoying a sunrise before?"

"With what intent?" he asked, his tone brittle.

She frowned at the mistrust in his voice. "If you think after all I have been through in the past day that I would jump and harm myself, then you do not know me very well."

They stood together in silence a moment before he sighed. "You are right. Perhaps we should change that." He came to stand beside her, gazing at the sunrise. "This is my favourite time of day. Each sunrise is different. And the colours . . . they are so beautiful."

Was he expecting her to reveal her deepest thoughts to him? All night long Rosalyn had wondered why all the MacLeods were being so nice to her. It made her wonder what they were hiding. There had to be a reason she had been warned against the Scots all her life, even though the ones who had cautioned her knew she was half-Scot as well. "I have no idea what you want me to say to you. We are supposed to be enemies."

"Are we?" He turned to look at her. "Or are we just two people who were placed on this earth at the same time? I have already told you I mean you no harm. You are free to leave if that is what you would like. And yet this morning instead of leaving, you came out here to watch the sunrise. It appears that perhaps instead of being enemies, we might as well find common ground."

"Such as what?" she asked, still suspicious of him and his family.

His gaze connected with hers in an unsettling way. "Do you trust me?"

She hesitated to answer as she twisted her hands before her. What was he asking her?

He held out his hand. "It is an aye or nay question."

She swallowed roughly. "I could trust you, but it depends entirely on what you are asking of me."

He reached for her hand, holding it gently, allowing her to pull away if that was what she chose. "Come with me. I do not think you will be disappointed."

With a hitch of her breath, she allowed Keiran to lead her back into the castle and down a long hallway until they stopped once more outside the chapel. "I discovered this secret only yesterday." He pulled her inside and stepped back towards the side of the chapel, then released her hand as his gaze lifted. "Have you ever seen anything so beautiful?"

Rosalyn's breath caught at the sight before her. The morning sun streamed in through the yellow and gold stained-glass window above the altar, bathing the entire chamber in a golden hue. But the light was not stagnant. The lead lines between the glass made the light dynamic—as though gliding through the chamber like water over pebbles.

Instantly, she was transported back to that moment in the forest when she had died. Her essence had left her body to hover over herself.

She is an abomination. The English soldier who had stabbed her said. *The world is better off without her.*

It was then that Keiran rose up, striking the man down. The colours of the rainbow surrounded him as he hurried back to her side and, placing his hands on her chest, brought her back to life.

A ripple of sensation moved down her spine as the light from her memory merged with the light in the chapel. *Light.* It was essential to all life, and a symbol of hope and guidance, knowledge and understanding, wisdom and truth, and love. At the moment of her death, light had flared from within Keiran himself, not from an outside source.

Was that light a sign from heaven above? Was Keiran her enemy, or was he pure goodness that could only have come from God? She turned around the chamber, taking in the light but also the idea that Keiran had been sent to her in a time of great need. And if so, she had no reason not to trust him.

"It is incredible," she finally said when she could voice words again. "I had no idea you could use light in such a way." She turned to Keiran and for a heartbeat, she saw the rainbow of colours that had surrounded him in the forest. She blinked and the light was no longer there. "Thank you for sharing this with me."

"Sharing my discoveries with you makes them even more special," he admitted. "My brothers and sisters have no doubt discovered the secrets of Dunvegan and witnessed them many times. Yet all this is new to me . . . and to you."

At his words, she frowned. "Until this moment, I do not

think I realised how much of an outsider you are to your own family."

He shrugged. "I have only just returned to them. Many of their ways are still unfamiliar to me, and there are many skills I have never learned that they all hold in high esteem."

"Like reading and writing?" she asked softly.

He nodded. "Among other things."

Rosalyn straightened. "I want to help you learn how to read and write, and anything else I might impart to you from my own limited education as a female."

He frowned. "You were not educated as your brother was?"

"I was allowed to participate in his lessons only until my parents died. Then my brother approved only of me studying music." She couldn't hide the smile that came to her lips. "But that did not stop me from sneaking into the study in the middle of the night to read from his books. Since I already knew how to read and write, I was able to teach myself Greek and Latin, mathematics, history, and geography."

Keiran's eyes widened. "That is impressive."

"I can teach all of that to you, if you'll allow it."

He nodded. "Let us start lessons tomorrow at sunrise. Meet me at the courtyard wall and I will show you yet another secret place."

"You do not wish your family to know about your lessons?"

He shook his head. "If you do not mind, I would like to keep this between you and me for now."

"I understand. I know the feeling of being less than others. My brother made me feel that way daily."

"Why was he forcing you to marry an Englishman stationed in Scotland?"

She dropped her gaze to her midriff, where the wound she'd sustained had fully healed. "I am not ready to share that story yet."

"I understand," he said echoing her earlier words.

Rosalyn pressed her lips together as her thoughts shifted back to the woods, the men who had attacked her, and the sword that had pierced her body. "I was dying. I know that for a fact. I felt it in every part of my soul." She brought her gaze back to Keiran's. "How did you heal me and help me survive? Warmth flowed from your hands into my body. I remember that part clearly, though not much else."

Keiran was about to respond when a white mist suddenly appeared in the doorway. *There you two are. I could feel your presence but not your exact location,* Lady Janet said with a hint of sorrow. *I do believe that in becoming more human, I have lost some of my abilities.*

Rosalyn held back a cry of distress as she scurried behind Keiran, trying to make herself as small as possible as the ghostly image floated forward. Why was Keiran not afraid?

"Mother," he greeted, then looked back at Rosalyn. "She will not hurt you. Come see," he said, offering his hand.

It is all right, child. I mean you no harm.

Rosalyn looked over Keiran's shoulder to see a grey fe-male figure that in the shifting morning light could look either translucent or solid, though she moved about not on legs, but on a floating grey mist. Rosalyn ignored Keiran's outstretched hand as she straightened and came to stand beside him. "You can talk? How is this possible?"

"Do not try to understand it. Just accept all this for what it is . . . a miracle." Keiran smiled at Rosalyn. "My mother died many years ago, but by the power of her love, she is still with us." As he turned back to the ghost, his smile slipped. "My brothers have led me to believe that you often present yourself when there is some sort of danger. Is that why you are here?"

Aye, my son. I can sense someone is coming.

"The English?" Keiran tensed.

Aye and nay. Two Englishmen are close, but they do not come for the MacLeods. The grey ghost turned towards Rosalyn. *They come for her.*

Rosalyn drew a shaky breath. "For me?"

Keiran's eyes turned stormy. "I made certain no one fol-lowed us yesterday. How could anyone possibly know you are here? God's blood. We need to tell Alastair so that he can enhance the castle's security." He took one of Rosalyn's hands in his own. "No one will get to you. Not here behind these walls."

Had those who had tried to kill her yesterday come back

to finish the task? Her free hand balled into a fist before she could force herself to relax. She had to believe she was safe with the MacLeods. Thinking any other way would only make her feel more defeated and alone than ever before.

You are not alone.

Rosalyn started at the words that invaded her thoughts. Keiran must have heard them too for he nodded as if in agreement. "You can read my thoughts?"

I can read your thoughts and sense your fear, Rosalyn de Clare. My son is right, you are safe for now, but he must alert the laird to the coming danger. The ghost shifted left and right, her agitation growing. *Keiran, my son, it is not only the English who come. There is another. I cannot tell for certain who it is, but I sense fairy blood.*

"Fairy blood? Why would—" Rosalyn started to ask, but when Keiran's expression hardened, the rest of her words died on her tongue.

"I thought I would have more time." Keiran's jaw tightened. "Come, Rosalyn. We must find Alastair and warn him of what may lie ahead." Keiran encouraged her to fall in step with him as he left the chapel and returned to the keep. The ghost trailed close behind them.

"What is it, Keiran? What is wrong?" Rosalyn asked, as she hurried to keep up with his longer stride.

"I had hoped beyond hope that I would have a long period of peace and contentment here at Dunvegan, but that is not to be if I am correct about the challenge before us."

What challenge? What could be worse than a patrol of angry Englishmen who wanted to smite her from this earth?

The fairy king, my dear, the ghost answered in her thoughts. *An angry, vengeful fairy who was bested by the MacLeods and now wants revenge.*

SOMETHING HAD SENSED his presence in the spirit realm. Oberon paused, floating in the in-between spaces of that world. He still did not have the strength to break free and emerge into the human realm, but he would once his body completed the final stage of regeneration. He still had to punish all the fairies who had helped to vaporise every part of him—body and spirit—into the nether regions, but that could wait until he took revenge on the MacLeods.

Aria, Graeme, Pearl, and Gille—with the help of the fairies—had almost destroyed him. They would have succeeded if he hadn't used all his magic to shield his soul from obliteration. With that one small part of himself intact, he had been able to draw residual amounts of life force from others in the underworld until his fairy form had returned. He wasn't as he had once been, but his translucent form was a step in the right direction. He would be whole again, in time. For now, it was enough that he'd been able to shift from the underworld into the spirit realm.

He would continue to gather what life force he could

from the spirits trapped in this realm with him, and once he gathered enough energy into his form, he could transform back to the being he had been for centuries. Fairy magic could change shape, but it could not be eliminated, he had learned from this experience. But the humans and fairies who had dared to cross him, and who were nowhere near as powerful as he, would rue the day he became whole again.

Anticipation flared inside Oberon as he floated in the timeless space that held him. It would not do to simply kill those who had crossed him. He wanted to make them suffer as he had, to feel the torment he'd experienced as he floated in an eternity of nothingness. He would take back the precious Fairy Flag, then strike the MacLeods and make them writhe, beg, and finally welcome their own deaths to stop the misery Oberon would deliver.

With a renewed sense of power, he swirled in the mist that held him. Hunger for revenge raked his soul. Very soon, he would once again take shape, and then he would be unstoppable.

CHAPTER EIGHT

A S THEY HURRIED towards the great hall, Keiran cursed himself for a fool. He should have told Rosalyn about Lieutenant James Long's plans to end her life rather than to marry her. But Keiran had not wanted to ruin that shared moment of joy between himself and Rosalyn. He clenched his jaw and increased his speed, forcing Rosalyn to keep up. Now two men were after her, no doubt wanting to finish what they had started. She had to know the truth, and he should be the one to tell her.

Keiran stopped abruptly, causing Rosalyn to crash into him. He gripped her arms to keep her from falling, and for a heartbeat allowed himself to enjoy the softness of the feminine body pressed so intimately against his own. A hint of lemon and rosemary filled his senses. Instead of releasing her, Keiran held her close, drawing in her scent. He was used to fairies smelling like flowers, not this sweet yet earthy combination.

"What is it?" Rosalyn asked, her eyes wide.

His mother had stopped as well, hovering behind Rosalyn. Setting her away from him, Keiran released

Rosalyn's arms. "I should have told you this earlier, but I simply must tell you now, before we meet with the others."

"You need not hide things from me." She steeled herself. "I have suffered enough hurt and rejection at my brother's hand. I've learned to be strong as a result."

He did not doubt that. It was better he simply stated the fact than try to soften the blow. "The soldier we captured revealed that your betrothed was behind the attack on your life. He meant to kill you, not marry you. He may try to continue what he started by sending the two men foretold by my mother." His gaze probed Rosalyn's.

She looked away, but not before he saw her features tighten with pain. "It matters not. With your help I escaped that fate. As far as I am concerned, I died yesterday, and was born anew, therefore releasing Lieutenant James Long from any obligation."

"Will he see things the same way?" Keiran asked.

She glanced back at him. "He will once I write and inform him thusly."

"And your brother?"

"He wanted only to be rid of me. I don't think he cared how he accomplished that goal." She stiffened and turned away, as though afraid to look at him.

Keiran studied her downcast face. She was hanging on to her self-control by a thread, trying so hard to be invincible. But he could see past her façade. The scared, lonely woman standing before him tore at his heart. He recalled his own loneliness in Fairyland when he'd been aged enough to register such an emotion. He remembered those first lonely nights, staring into the darkness, wondering what was to become of him. Aye, he understood her fear, but he also applauded her bravery. It took great courage to remain in the house of her enemy and act as though nothing he said could break her.

An almost aching tenderness unfolded within him. He wanted to reach out to her, to reassure her with a gentle touch that she was not as alone as she imagined. "Rosalyn?" Her name, spoken so gently, hung between them. Slowly, she lifted her gaze to his. In her eyes, he saw a faint, hesitant stirring of hope. "Those men will never get close to you. I will make certain of that."

"Why would you protect me when my own people will not?" The morning light illuminated her pale skin, accentuating her freckles and the lines of worry bracketing her mouth.

Her question caught him off guard. He had learned in Fairyland that even taken away from his clan, the essence of who he was had remained. He was a protector of all living things, even this female—even his enemy. "I need you to remain here, and alive, if you are to be my tutor."

"Of course. Good tutors are difficult to come by, even in England. I can understand going out of your way to keep me safe. It would be such a nuisance to have to replace me."

The sting of sarcasm was not lost on him. His lips

quirked, as did her own briefly before slowly fading until pain once again darkened her hazel eyes. She stood so close to him, and yet she remained somehow separate. Alone and untouchable. Yet in the moment, he finally understood. She was used to the world attacking her, catching her unprepared, betraying her at every turn. She expected him to betray her as well. After all, in her mind, he was her enemy.

Keiran stepped forward, and reached for her hand, wrapping her cold fingers with his own warmer ones. "I do appreciate that you have agreed to tutor me, but your presence here at Dunvegan is not just one of convenience. I want you here. I like having you here because . . . I do not have many friends in this world, and I would like it very much if you would be that for me. A friend."

Her eyes widened. "You want to be friends? With me, an Englishwoman?"

"Since your mother was also of Scottish blood, then that makes you not fully English. And since I was born a Scot but raised elsewhere, that makes me not fully Scottish." He shrugged. "I suspect we have as good a chance as any at friendship."

Her brows came together but a lightness entered her eyes. "If we are to be friends, then you must be honest with me in all things."

He nodded. "I will hold nothing back no matter how desperate the situation."

She paused, thinking, then nodded. "What do I have to

lose? My only family has washed his hands of me. My once betrothed tried to kill me. I have no future unless I can find employment as a tutor. I suppose being friends with you cannot make things any worse, now, could it?"

"I do not suppose it could." He gave her hand a light squeeze, then released her fingers, and instead offered her his arm. "Shall we go tell my brother what Mother has sensed?"

At the reminder that Lady Janet was behind them, they both turned towards the spirit. Instead of the distress that had darkened her features, a smile lit her face. *I am glad you two found common ground. A bond forged when enemies become friends is stronger than any other.*

They were never truly enemies, were they? Keiran pondered as he led Rosalyn and his mother inside the castle, and up the stairs. Both male and female voices came to them as they moved down the hallway and entered the great hall. The entire family was gathered as they had just finished breaking their morning fast.

At the sight of all the MacLeods, Rosalyn pulled away from Keiran and clutched her hands before her. He understood. She was ready to think of him differently, but the rest of his clan still had to prove themselves.

"Come, join us," Gwendolyn said, motioning them towards the table where she and Alastair sat with Tormod, Orrick, Graeme, Fiona, Isolde, and Aria.

Keiran waited until Rosalyn was seated next to Isolde before he took a seat next to Orrick. Lady Janet followed more slowly as she took a moment to hug each of her children, as that ability had been restored to her thanks to Aria's residual magic.

Gwendolyn scooped helpings of oatmeal porridge into two bowls and passed them down to Rosalyn and Keiran. The cream followed.

Keiran dressed his oats and scooped them up quickly. Even so, he savoured the sweetness of the cream and the nutty flavour of the oats. Rosalyn brought the spoon to her lips, tasting the porridge tentatively.

Keiran frowned. "Have you never had oats before?"

She shook her head. "My breakfast usually consisted of toast and jam with a spot of tea."

"Eat the oats," Orrick advised. "You'll need something more substantial to keep you warm as the springtime air holds a chill here in Scotland."

At Keiran's nod, she took another bite. "They are quite tasty."

Gwendolyn smiled. "Break your fast, then Alastair is planning to take you, Keiran, to Knock Castle to start your training as our estate manager. The castle is turning into a ruin, but perhaps some attention from you can salvage it for the next generation of MacLeods."

"We cannot," Keiran replied. "There is something more urgent that must be attended to."

Alastair pushed his bowl of porridge aside. "Of what do you speak?"

"Mother warned me that two Englishmen are near Dunvegan. They seek Rosalyn."

Alastair tossed a look at his brothers. "Then it is up to us to find them first." Alastair, Tormod, Orrick, and Graeme stood but Keiran waved them back to their seats.

"There is more," he said, his fingers tightening on his spoon. "I fear it is only a matter of time before Oberon returns to challenge us."

Tormod frowned and leaned forward. "How could you know this?"

"Mother felt his presence."

The colour drained from Aria's already pale face. "I felt that, too, but did not want to believe it was true."

"How can this be?" Gwendolyn asked. "You destroyed him."

"Fairy magic destroyed his body but now we know it did not destroy his essence. It would take time for him to regenerate."

"How long?" Alastair asked.

Aria shrugged. "It depends on the resources available to him. A few days, weeks, months. We cannot be certain."

Alastair's lips set in a grim line. "Then we had best take care of the Englishmen quickly so we can turn our attention to Oberon."

Gwendolyn left her seat and moved to a chest of drawers against the wall. Opening a drawer, she withdrew something before returning to the table where she held out an iron bracelet to Rosalyn. "Take this and wear it always. It will protect you from fairy magic."

Rosalyn accepted the gift with a frown. "Is this necessary? How much power can one fairy possess?"

"Aye, you must wear the bracelet." Keiran took it from her and secured it around her right wrist before pulling back his sleeve to reveal his own band clamped tight around his wrist. "We all wear them because the last time we went up against Oberon, he almost took the lives of all the MacLeods and everyone living within these castle walls."

Rosalyn's other hand came up to wrap around the simple iron adornment. "This will stop him from touching anyone not fae?"

"It will not stop him, but it will help minimise the control he will have over you. It will protect you from a personal assault from anyone else in the fairy realm who is not as strong as Oberon," Keiran assured her, though his words did not ease the concern that tightened her features. He didn't blame her. The fairy realm was difficult for most humans to understand if they had not had interactions with those beings. The two men who his mother claimed were after her were no doubt a more urgent threat. Turning to Alastair he said, "We should assemble a search party and find the Englishmen while the information we attained from the Nicolson clan about where the English were stationed is still valid."

"My thought exactly. Tormod, Orrick, Graeme, Aria?

Would you like to join Keiran and myself?"

Tormod nodded.

"Aria and I should hold back and keep watch over the castle's defences," Orrick said as he and Aria stood.

"Very well," Alastair agreed. "We do not know what we are up against yet."

Gwendolyn rose and came to stand beside Rosalyn. "I will watch over Rosalyn," she said with a smile. "Besides, our seamstress has discovered a few lengths of fabric in a chest. I asked her to measure you for two new gowns."

Rosalyn turned to look at Gwendolyn. "You have been more than generous with the gowns I received last night. I could not possibly impose."

"'Tis not an imposition," Gwendolyn assured her. "We have plenty to share." Her gaze moved past Rosalyn to the other women seated at the table before returning to Rosalyn.

At the determined look on Gwendolyn's face, Rosalyn finally nodded, stood, then quietly followed Gwendolyn from the hall. The other women followed.

A wave of relief swept through Keiran that Rosalyn would remain safely behind the stone walls of Dunvegan while he and his brothers searched for the Englishmen who threatened her. "When do we leave?" Keiran asked, straightening, and searching the other men's faces.

As the men stood, and Alastair moved off to gather warriors to assist them on the quest, Keiran stared at the doorway through which Gwendolyn and Rosalyn had vanished. He marvelled at the changes in Rosalyn since yesterday, when she had been like a frightened, injured, and angry kitten. Today, she held her head high, despite the fact she was surrounded by strangers. And when his mother had proclaimed she was the target of the Englishmen's hunt, she had not shown fear.

"Which direction shall we head?" Graeme asked, interrupting Keiran's thoughts. "You said you were the strategist for Oberon in Fairyland. Perhaps your skills can help us figure out how to proceed without having to divide ourselves into two groups."

"If the men are coming from the same area where Rosalyn was attacked near Struan, then we should head to the north-east. Unless they have a boat, they will be forced to go around Loch Caroy."

"And if they have a boat?" Tormod asked with a frown.

"The likelihood of that is very low, but if they do, then we will be heading in the wrong direction."

"I say we split up and cover both," Tormod challenged.

Keiran should have expected such a response from Tormod. His brother did not like to fail, would do anything to avoid it, in fact. "I am told Mother's premonitions are not always accurate. She saw two men, but perhaps there are more. Why weaken our defences by dividing our numbers?"

"I agree with Keiran," Alastair said, coming to join them. "We stay together. If we are to face an entire regiment of men, then we will need all of us to defend ourselves. And we will all need Keiran if something should go wrong."

At Keiran's puzzled expression, Alastair added, "Your powers of healing give us an edge we have never had before. 'Tis a gift we shall protect and cherish."

Alastair signalled for the men to mount, and as they headed towards the open gates, he brought his horse alongside Keiran's. "It only now occurred to me, but when you heal someone, is there a cost to yourself?"

Keiran nodded. "I grow weak, and depending on the severity of the wound, sometimes it takes a while for my strength to return."

"That is good to know. If we are forced to use your healing, we will protect you while you recover," Alastair said, increasing the pace as he guided the men to the north-east.

Keiran increased his speed to stay with Alastair. "You realise I have never tested my abilities on more than a few broken bones and gashes from swords. I truly have no idea of the extent of my abilities or the long-term effects on my person."

"I understand, Keiran. But a chance at life after a deadly battle is better than no chance at all. Judging by the blood on Rosalyn's gown, her injury was substantial. You brought her back from the edge of death. I hope you would do the same for one of your brothers."

"Of course, but isn't it better to avoid a bloody conflict than to test my abilities? Besides, Orrick led me to believe you were the one who wanted to negotiate peace instead of fight. What has changed?"

"I was able to keep the peace between the clans and the Scottish government, which is always trying to exert more control over the clans. But the English are an entirely different enemy. They outnumber us, they have resources that we do not, and they are growing less tolerant of our way of life here in the Highlands. To the English, those who support the Hanoverians are good, and those who still support the Stuarts are evil," Alastair said. "The day is coming when we MacLeods will have to choose a side and take a stand against those who oppose us."

Politics was not something Keiran knew much about, having been raised in Fairyland. Though, in the last few weeks he had heard his brothers talking about the Jacobite cause and the threat of invasion from England. Keiran frowned as he stared into the distance. He had not realised, until that moment, the weight Alastair carried as laird. Not only was he responsible for managing his estates, which included collecting rents, maintaining roads and bridges, and providing food and shelter for his tenants, he also had to balance his relationship with the Scottish government and the other clan lairds. All while trying to keep his people safe from the constant threat of English invasion. And now they faced the added threat of what Oberon would do to them all once he emerged.

No wonder Alastair was so keen on the idea that Keiran could heal his people if injured. It gave him one less worry.

"I will gladly help where I am able," Keiran replied. "With healing and with your estates."

"Thank you, Keiran." Alastair smiled at his brother before turning his gaze back to the path ahead.

Keiran narrowed his gaze on the landscape as they passed, searching for anything out of the ordinary. Discovering and detaining the Englishmen who threatened Rosalyn was urgent. Only then would they get back to finding a means to rid themselves of Oberon before the fairy king regained his powers. An English invasion would not matter to the MacLeods if Oberon destroyed them all first.

CHAPTER NINE

ROSALYN STARED AT the stone walls as her heartbeat thudded in her ears while she, Aria, Gwendolyn, Fiona, and Isolde walked silently down the hallway. They moved down the stairs, and into a strange room with weapons displayed on every wall, causing her heart to jump. Was this it? Fear roared, renewed within her. Was this the end of her life? And it would come at the hands of the women of the castle instead of the men? Her mind raced with unanswered questions.

The air in the chamber was sweet, laced with the scent of the sea, yet it wrapped around her like a shroud. It was suddenly thick and lifeless as it covered her nose and mouth, pressing against her lungs, suffocating her with the memory of the men attacking her in the woods. She drew a gasping breath and glanced around wildly, searching for the door, for Keiran, for anything that would save her.

A gentle touch came to her arm, and she jerked towards the sensation. "Do not be afraid, Rosalyn. We are here to help you, not hurt you."

She saw a beautiful white-haired woman standing before

her with a look of concern bringing a crease to her otherwise perfect brow. Aria. Rosalyn shook her head, clearing it of her imaginings. She recognised the woman and then Isolde, Gwendolyn, and Fiona who stood close beside her.

"We did not mean to frighten you," Aria said. "Our goal is to empower you."

"With a dress fitting, here in this room?" She looked about her again, recognising the chamber as that of an armoury.

"The poor dear is still traumatised from her near-death experience yesterday," Fiona said in a compassionate tone. "We should have prepared ahead of time about our little deception."

"Deception?" Rosalyn's heart and breathing stuttered again. "Are you here to kill me or not?"

"Heavens, no!" Aria exclaimed with a chuckle. "We are here to teach you how to defend yourself. None of us had any idea as to what weapon you might be most skilled at, so we thought coming here would help expedite discovering that."

"But the dress fitting?" Rosalyn asked, still confused by what they had led her to believe.

"Our seamstress already knows your measurements since the gowns we gave you yesterday fit so well. We did not mislead you about that. She is creating two new gowns for you as we speak. They should be ready by tomorrow at the latest. But before we get to why we are here, I have a few questions for you."

"Such as?" Rosalyn asked hesitantly.

"You are betrothed to Lieutenant James Long?" Gwendolyn asked.

At Rosalyn's nod, she continued, "Did you sign a betrothal document?"

"No. Why do you ask?" Rosalyn frowned. "My brother took care of all the arrangements."

Gwendolyn's features brightened. "That is excellent. Though I have one last question. Was the betrothal ever consummated?"

Rosalyn could feel heat rush to her cheeks. "Never. All I did was kiss the man once. And that one mistake almost cost me my life."

"I apologise for asking such personal questions," Gwendolyn said with a gentle smile. "I think I have someone who can help you. He is a friend of Callum's, Geordie Buchannan, a solicitor. He was able to help Alastair and me when we had our own betrothal problems."

"But you married Alastair." Rosalyn curled her fingers into a tight ball, trying not to let hope blossom. Only pain and disappointment had ever occurred.

"We were betrothed and about to marry when I was kidnapped and hidden away with my siblings for five long years. In that time, Alastair attached himself to another woman, and when I returned, we had to sort out that muddle. Geordie was very helpful. I sent a message for him to come to Dunvegan. I do hope he can help you as well."

"Thank you," Rosalyn said, her voice tight as the hope that had threatened broke free. The thought that she might someday be legally free of the lieutenant brought a smile to her lips.

"No thanks are necessary. Someone helped me in a time of need, I am happy to help you in yours." Gwendolyn moved to the wall and took down a sword. "Now, we should return to the reason we came to this chamber."

"Aye," Isolde said as she retrieved a bow and a quiver of arrows.

Fiona took down a dagger, and Aria took down a crossbow. "Have you ever used any of these weapons before?" Aria asked.

"No. My brother never let me anywhere near his weapons. In England, gentlemen do not wear swords as often as they do here," Rosalyn replied.

"We suspected as much," Aria said. "Let us go outside and see which of these weapons you might have a natural talent for using. Shall we?" She guided them out of the chamber and to the rear courtyard.

Outside, gusts of cool morning air brushed past Rosalyn's cheeks. She still wasn't certain what the women had in mind as far as teaching her anything to do with weapons, and she marvelled that they would even think to arm their enemy with any means to harm them. "Why are you doing this?"

All four women turned to her with curious expressions, but it was Isolde who stepped forward and offered her the bow. She drew an arrow and handed it to Rosalyn. "Each of us knows what it is to feel powerless, to be a victim of circumstance. We do not want that for you."

"We all learned to fight against those who tried to keep us from becoming who we are now," Gwendolyn said. "We don't want you to be in the same situation where you found yourself yesterday, at the mercy of those who would harm you, with no way to defend yourself."

"I tried to fight them. They were too powerful. There were too many of them," Rosalyn admitted, feeling a sense of relief at finally being able to talk about her experience. "If Keiran had not come along, I would have died."

"That is why we are here with you now," Fiona said with a smile. "You will never find yourself in that situation again after today."

Rosalyn straightened, feeling not only gratitude, but a sense of growing excitement that she might learn how to be more independent in her new life. "I am ready to learn." She lifted the bow and tried to put the arrow to it. She fumbled and the arrow fell to the ground.

"Let me show you," Isolde said, standing behind Rosalyn and helping her hold the bow steady before setting the arrow against the string of the bow. Isolde positioned her fingers so that one sat above the arrow and two were below. "Pull the string back until it touches your lips and chin, and aim at the

wall in the distance. Keep your arm straight, but not stiff."
Isolde stepped back. "When you are ready, relax your string
hand and the arrow will fly straight and true," she said in an
encouraging tone.

Rosalyn drew a slow, even breath and relaxed the string.
The tension in the string surprised her and she jerked back,
sending the arrow not at the wall, but straight into the air. As
it came down, the women scattered to keep from being
struck.

"That was good for your first attempt," Isolde said, with
slightly less encouragement than before. "Try again."

The next three attempts held similar, dangerous results.

"Instead of running for our lives," Aria said, interrupting
a fourth attempt, "let's try something new." She took the
bow and handed Rosalyn a crossbow. "Perhaps this light-
weight crossbow from the Middle Ages is more your style. It
is old, but very dependable."

Rosalyn accepted the weapon and was a bit surprised at
how light it was. "How do I use it?"

"First, you press the trigger underneath." While Rosalyn
held the crossbow, Aria coached her. "Bring the nut forward
so that it can accept the leather string when you pull it
back." Rosalyn did and tried to pull the string, but it barely
moved.

Aria held up a strange-looking metal tool. "You cannot
move it with your hands. Brace the bow against your leg and
use the goat's foot lever." Aria motioned for Rosalyn to slip

the lever's feet into the metal rungs on the side of the bolt. "Make certain the hook catches on the leather string, then pull back. You'll hear a click when you have done it correctly. Remove the tool and tuck it into your belt."

Rosalyn looked at her waist. "I do not have a belt."

Aria pressed her lips together, no doubt trying to control her patience with all Rosalyn's fumbling. "If this weapon works for you, we'll find you a belt. Now, set a bolt against the string. These bolts have feathers, but bolts can also use leather or parchment to help guide their flight. Lift the weapon and sight your enemy over the top, then depress the trigger."

The bolt sailed across the courtyard and struck the wall before falling to the ground. "That's better," Aria exclaimed. "Try it again, this time by yourself."

Rosalyn was encouraged that the bolt at least went in the direction she had desired. Determined to succeed a second time, she tried to do as she had been instructed only to drop the weapon several times before finally setting a bolt against the string. When she took aim, the bolt did fly where she had planned. Expecting praise, she was surprised to see a frown on Aria's face.

"You must be faster. The enemy had time to plunder you and everyone around you." Aria shook her head and removed the crossbow from Rosalyn's hands.

"Never fear," Gwendolyn said. "This is a short sword because it is half the size of the longswords the men usually use. It is easier for a female to use. Move your wrist around and see how it feels in your grip. Think of it as an extension of your arm. Take two steps forward and thrust, then two steps back and block," Gwendolyn instructed, showing Rosalyn how to move.

Rosalyn took the weapon. It felt heavy in her hands, and certainly not a part of her arm. She moved around the courtyard, sending the women scattering. Instead of making her feel empowered, she felt awkward and off balance as she moved forward and back. But more than that, it put the enemy close to her. *Too close.* She stopped and turned to the women with a sigh of defeat. "I'm not certain I can look someone in the eyes and thrust this weapon into their body. Women were meant to give life, not take it."

Fiona placed a hand over her abdomen. "Creating life means nothing if you cannot protect it from harm."

Gwendolyn drew a sharp breath as she beamed at the red-haired woman.

"Oh, Fiona, does that mean what I think it means?" Isolde asked with a smile.

Fiona smiled and nodded. "I suspected I was with child, but I was not certain until this morning when Lottie confirmed my suspicions."

"We are so happy for you and Tormod," Aria said, her tone filled with good humour.

As the three women fussed over Fiona, Rosalyn continued to watch them, and admiration mixed with jealousy inside her chest, weighing her down. These women clearly supported each other in both good and bad times if their familiarity with weapons was any indication. She had never had that kind of support in her life from anyone. What would it be like to share her darkest fears and brightest hopes with these women? They were all so different in both looks and talents, and yet so much alike in their care and generosity towards each other.

Rosalyn craved such connection. These women had taken her into their circle, even knowing she was English. They did not know about her own Scottish heritage; only Keiran knew that.

Gwendolyn broke away from the group and came towards Rosalyn. "Our apologies. We were not trying to exclude you from sharing in Fiona's joy, though she made an excellent point." Gwendolyn concentrated on the blade in Rosalyn's hands. "We cannot give life and then not protect it. That protection extends from my children to everyone I love. You will find you will do whatever is necessary to protect what is important to you . . . including your own life in the heat of battle." She brought her gaze to Rosalyn's. "Isn't it better to learn how to protect yourself and others and never need that knowledge than to not know how, and wish you had learned?"

"Yes," Rosalyn agreed. Had she had a weapon during her attack yesterday, she had no doubt she would have used it to keep that man from stabbing her. "I want to learn. Please do not give up on me."

"Never," Fiona said, taking the sword from Rosalyn's hands and replacing it with a dagger. "This dagger has taken many lives, but it has saved them as well. It is a balance: life and death. We are not asking you to take lives needlessly, only to decide if this weapon should be used when there is no other option."

Rosalyn wrapped her hand around the hilt. The stone warmed in her hand. "How would I use this weapon?"

"Look at the blade," Fiona instructed. "Notice that one side is sharpened, but on the opposite side there is a blunt edge that can be used to brace against your body. This is a defensive weapon, and only used to slice or stab when necessary. You would use it with the sharpened side towards your body so that you can take those blows without damaging your blade. You reverse the blade like this to block." She moved the sword so that the blunt edge was braced against Rosalyn's forearm. "On the blunt side, only the top three inches of the blade are sharpened." She stepped back, allowing Rosalyn space to manoeuvre the dagger forward and backward, which she did with ease.

Fiona lifted the sword and came at her with a strike. Rosalyn easily blocked it and smiled. "This weapon feels more natural than all the others."

The women smiled at her. "Then we have found what will work for you should you need such a weapon. It is yours," Aria said, handing her a sheath. "Store it with the sharpened side up so when you draw it, you are ready to position it correctly."

Rosalyn frowned. "Where do I store it?" she asked, looking at the straps extending from the sheath.

They all laughed. "Looks like we are going to have to get you a belt after all," Aria said.

"When do I wear it?" Rosalyn asked, warming to the idea of carrying a weapon. "None of you have weapons on yourselves."

The women all lifted the hems of their skirts and pulled a small blade from their boots. "We will find a *sgian-dubh* for you as well," Aria said, lifting her skirt higher, revealing a leather sheath strapped to her leg. "If you are comfortable wearing the dagger, I can have a leg sheath made for you, or else you will leave it in your chamber until you know there is a threat or anytime you leave this castle."

"Thank you." Rosalyn smiled at the women gathered near her. "As your e—a stranger, you did not have to teach me, but I am so glad you did."

Gwendolyn's brows came together. "You are not a stranger, and you are certainly not our enemy. You are our new friend, and we care about what happens to you."

Rosalyn's throat tightened. She could feel tears burning behind her eyes and quickly closed her lids to hide them. Gwendolyn's words touched her, but it was the sincerity in the woman's eyes that sent a spiral of warmth through her.

"Open your eyes, Rosalyn," Gwendolyn said.

She opened her eyes to find all four women smiling at her with that same look Gwendolyn's eyes held. It spoke of acceptance and friendship.

"When we look at you, we do not see an Englishwoman, we see someone who is strong and determined to rise above the hardships that have been thrown at her," Gwendolyn said, reaching for Rosalyn's hand. "You are a survivor, just as we all are. We share a bond, and with that bond you are now one of us."

This time Rosalyn could not stop the tears that came to her eyes. "You have no idea how much those words mean to me."

"We all understand how difficult it is to revisit the past, but if there comes a time when you want to talk about your brother, or why you were sent to Scotland, or anything else, we are here to listen," Fiona said, her tone filled with the acceptance Rosalyn had seen in her eyes.

"Again, I thank you for your understanding." The pressure in Rosalyn's chest eased as she looked from the women, past the walls of Dunvegan, and to the great expanse of the loch beyond. Yesterday her life had been all but at an end. Today it had started once more in the presence of these brave women and in the protection of the MacLeods.

A breeze that was cool but not chill brushed against her cheeks and tugged at her hair, bringing with it the heady scent of salt mixed with the emerging spring green and rich earth. Instead of fear she suddenly found herself filled with hope—hope that her life truly was starting over with these extraordinary women as her friends, and for a future that had yet to reveal itself but had nothing to do with either her brother or Lieutenant James Long.

CHAPTER TEN

KEIRAN RODE BESIDE Alastair as they made their way through the forestland. Their horses moved restlessly, their breath pluming in the cold morning air as each man searched the shadows made by the trees. Perhaps, based on the way the horses skittered, they sensed something the men did not. Keiran held up his hand, silently signalling for them all to stop.

In the silence Keiran listened. Nothing but the trickling of water in a nearby stream and birds chattering in the canopy above came to him. He narrowed his gaze, searching for something out of the ordinary, when finally he saw steam rising in the air like what the horses and they themselves generated, coming from behind a cluster of trees.

With a motion of his hand, Keiran signalled the direction and for the men to dismount and separate into two groups. One to head east, the other west, hopefully catching the hidden men unaware of their presence. Silently, Keiran drew his sword, and crouched low as he crept forward. Alastair did the same behind him. He could see Tormod and Graeme on the opposite side, closing in on the location of the breathing vapours.

They were close, so close. Keiran leapt forward along with Tormod, only to have four grazing deer leap from the cover of the shrubs and race into the distance.

In that same moment, two men sprang up from the foliage, their swords ready to strike. Keiran cursed himself for a fool that he had fallen for such a trick and lifted his sword to meet the blow aimed at his head. The sound of steel meeting steel echoed through the forest as the men who had attacked suddenly realised they were outnumbered. The man before Keiran turned and ran. Keiran pursued.

The man sprinted ahead, leaping over branches, ducking and weaving around pine and rowan trees that slowed his brothers down, but Keiran was used to running through the woods in Fairyland. The muscles in his thighs stretched as his legs pumped, propelling him through the forest, his stare intent on the man ahead of him.

He was closing in on his prey, his body responding to his every demand. He could run like this for hours without tiring, but he would need only one more moment to catch his enemy. Keiran was close enough now to hear the man's laboured breathing as he leapt over a log. Keiran reached out to graze the man's arm, but the man surged ahead, his muddy dark blue aura indicating his fear.

Keiran's senses heightened as he ran faster. The sun's rays filtered through the canopy above, casting dappled shadows on the ground as his feet pounded against the soft earth. He noted a slight twitch of the man's head, indicating he would head right, towards the loch in the distance. Anticipating the shift, Keiran reached out just as he turned, grabbing then yanking his enemy against his body. They fell together onto the mossy forest floor. Grabbing the man's wrists, Keiran raised them up over his head as he pinned the man beneath him.

The man glared as he thrashed beneath Keiran's body.

"Surrender," Keiran demanded.

"I would rather die than surrender to you," the man spat at Keiran.

"That can be arranged," Keiran said, rising off the man and dragging him to his feet. He secured the man's hands behind him with a length of rope he drew from his sporran, just as Alastair skidded to a stop beside them.

"I had no idea you were so fast," Alastair said between harsh breaths. "From now on you can chase all our enemies."

"Did Tormod and Graeme catch the other one?" Keiran asked, leading their prisoner back the way they had come.

"I have no idea," Alastair said. "I was so focused on trying to keep up with you I lost sight of them."

The man dragged his feet, slowing their progress forward. "I asked you to kill me rather than take me prisoner."

A wry chuckle escaped Keiran. "We are not going to kill you unless you refuse to answer our questions. For starters, why were you on MacLeod land?"

"I cannot tell you." The man scowled. "No matter what I

say, death awaits me." His aura darkened. "Please, I beg you to end my life now before he does."

"He?" Keiran asked as he and Alastair shared a glance. "We can protect you if you tell us what we need to know."

"No, you can't. You MacLeods have no idea who you are up against." From his grasp on the man's arm, Keiran could feel the man trembling. Who was this man so afraid of?

Once again Keiran shared a glance with Alastair. "The sooner we return to Dunvegan, the better," Alastair said.

"Agreed." Keiran forced the man up onto the saddle of his horse before mounting behind him. They only had to wait a few moments before Graeme and Tormod arrived with their prisoner.

"This one did not even put up a fight," Graeme said, as Tormod secured the second prisoner on his horse.

The man's black aura indicated negative emotions such as anger or resentment. Both fear and resentment were normal responses to the situation in which the men had found themselves. There was no indication of deception, for which Keiran was grateful, yet he still wanted to hurry back to the protective walls of Dunvegan with all due haste.

As they rode, Keiran clasped his muscular arm like a steel band around his enemy's waist. He had managed to find the men his mother had warned them about only hours ago, meaning Rosalyn was safe for now. At the thought warmth flared in his chest, along with something else he did not want to name.

BACK AT DUNVEGAN, the men took the two prisoners into two separate chambers. Alastair oversaw the interrogation of the man who was angry and resentful in the great hall, while Keiran and Tormod attempted to break the more fearful man in the old keep that was still being refurbished.

The room they were in had not yet been enclosed, and a light breeze rippled through the unfinished chamber. The man sat in the chair in which they had placed him with his arms crossed before him, refusing to look at either Keiran or Tormod. "Who sent you?" Keiran asked, his voice booming in the open space as he fisted his hands, trying to stay in control. He wanted answers and would do almost anything to get them.

The man's chin tilted up. He narrowed his eyes, the hate in them as sharp as a newly honed blade. "I have nothing to say to you."

Keiran walked in a tight circle around the man, forcing himself to breathe. The sooner they gained answers, the sooner he could go and check on Rosalyn to see how she fared in his absence. Tormod had asked Keiran not to use his powers to gain information from this man. His brother was worried that the more people who knew about his powers the more risk there would be for Keiran.

So instead, Keiran leaned close to the man's face and scowled. "Did Lieutenant James Long send you?"

The man's eyes went wide. "How did you know?" Then realising what he had acknowledged, he paled. "I meant, I do not know."

"The lieutenant relinquished his connection to his betrothed when he tried to kill her, so why does he want her now?" Keiran asked, his voice brusque.

The man flinched. "He will kill me for telling you this, but I suppose I am dead if I remain silent or tell you the truth." The man sighed, no doubt realising there was no retracting what he had admitted. "The lieutenant does not like to lose at anything, not at cards, in war, or in matters of the heart. He suspected the MacLeods were holding his betrothed hostage, which is why he sent us to confirm that fact. When we do not return, he will see that as confirmation of his suspicions, and will stop at nothing to get her back."

Keiran's stomach tightened. "He'll never get the chance to attack and wound Rosalyn a second time."

A confused expression settled on the man's brow but before he could speak, Keiran turned to Tormod. "I'll leave his fate up to you," Keiran said, before walking out of the chamber. He needed to speak to Alastair. Keiran understood enough about the human realm to know that a near-death experience was not enough to sever a betrothal contract. It might help expedite the process, but until Rosalyn was officially free of her intended, she was still Lieutenant James Long's property. And the MacLeods might have to go to war with the English to keep her safe. Keiran only hoped Alastair would agree to such a plan.

Keiran found Alastair in the library, sitting at his desk with a young man of medium height, with a square, hard jaw. At Keiran's entrance, the man rose and offered a bow.

"Keiran, you are just the person I was hoping to see," Alastair said, waving his brother towards the seat opposite him behind the desk. "This is Geordie Buchannan, our solicitor."

"A solicitor?" Keiran shifted his gaze between the two men, amazed at the man's presence. "How could you possibly know that was what I was coming to talk to you about?"

"Gwendolyn arranged for Geordie to come earlier today. I had no idea he was coming until a moment ago." Alastair leaned back in his chair. "My wife is clever, indeed."

"Agreed," said Keiran as he settled in his own chair.

The solicitor slipped on a pair of spectacles, then pulled a sheaf of papers close before picking up his quill. "I was led to believe there is yet another betrothal agreement that I am to try to dissolve?"

"We should send for Rosalyn," Keiran said, a heartbeat before she appeared at the door.

"Come in, Rosalyn," Alastair said, standing and moving to hold out the chair next to the solicitor for Rosalyn to sit before returning to his own chair. "Mr Buchannan is here to help you terminate the contract of your betrothal to Lieutenant Long, if that is what you wish."

"With all my heart," she said, turning her gaze to the young man beside her.

"I must ask you a few more questions. Gwendolyn already informed me about the particulars of your arrangement with Lieutenant Long." He positioned his quill over the paper. "Are you aware of a bride price being paid?"

Rosalyn shook her head. "There was no exchange to my knowledge. I had no dowry to offer."

The solicitor made a few notations on his paper. When he was done, he looked up once more. "And to be absolutely clear, you did not sign any sort of contract?"

Rosalyn lifted her chin and met the solicitor's gaze directly. "I signed nothing. My brother was the force behind this proposal. Had he asked my opinion, I would have refused."

The solicitor set his quill down and looked to Alastair. "Is there any proof that Lieutenant Long tried to harm Miss de Clare?"

"We retained her bloody clothing. The fabric of her gown is torn where the sword pierced her flesh," Alastair offered.

Keiran leaned forward. "I witnessed the event, and we have taken the man who stabbed her as our prisoner. He confessed that it was Long who sent him to kill her."

The solicitor picked up his quill and made several more notations before turning to Rosalyn. His gaze narrowed. "If you are called upon to show the courts your wound, are you prepared to do that?"

Her breath caught as she paled. "I cannot—"

"There is no need for her to expose herself," Keiran interrupted, not wanting Rosalyn to reveal that her wound no longer existed. Such a fact might support Long in suggesting that the situation never occurred. "A witness, the bloody clothing, and the attacker's confession should be sufficient evidence to support the dissolution of a poorly executed contract."

"It will entirely depend on the courts," the solicitor said. "I will have to travel to England to file the necessary documents, unless there is any reason they could be filed here in Scotland."

"Perhaps they should be filed here. Lieutenant Long's regiment is here, and . . ." She paused, looking down at her twined hands before unfurling them and smoothing them against her skirt. She drew a breath, raised her head, and said, "Mr Buchannan, my mother was Scottish and my father English, making me half-Scot."

Even though Keiran already knew that information after hearing her attacker's confession yesterday, she'd had yet to acknowledge that fact to any of them. Yet, she revealed her heritage now, not with shame, but with a hint of pride in her voice.

The solicitor's brow arched. "Thank you for sharing that information, Miss de Clare. That will make filing a petition much easier, and I'll be honest, the Scottish courts are much friendlier to the petitions of women than the English courts." Mr Buchannan took off his glasses, then gathered his papers and rose. "One last question. If there is a forfeiture price to be paid, are you able to pay that?"

"The MacLeods will cover all the expenses," Alastair said before she could reply, for which Keiran was grateful. He would have to thank Alastair later.

"Very well," the solicitor said. "Then I will be in touch soon."

Alastair rose and escorted the solicitor from the room, leaving Keiran and Rosalyn alone. Giving her time to recover from the questions the solicitor had asked, Keiran focused on the early afternoon sun as it slanted through the stained-glass window above the desk, painting the library floor in a patchwork of vibrant hues. Dust motes danced in the warm beams, and time itself seemed to slow. This space suddenly felt like a sanctuary, and he stopped trying to avoid the woman across the table from him, suddenly needing to know more about what she had admitted earlier. "Rosalyn, when you talked about your heritage, your voice tightened. Are you ashamed of being a Scot?"

As she turned, the sun caught her eyes. They weren't simply hazel. Instead, the light danced inside them, illuminating flecks of gold that made him recall the most beautiful fairies in Fairyland. Yet it wasn't simply her eyes that radiated beauty. A light came from within her as well, a light created from knowing defeat, suffering, struggle, and loss.

"After the death of my parents, I was taught that my Scottish heritage was something to be hidden so that others would not despise me or treat me differently. More recently, my brother warned me that to acknowledge our mother's past would only bring me heartache." A flash of pain darkened her eyes. "For once, my brother was right. Heartache, indeed. I am not certain anymore if I am more ashamed to be English or Scottish, and I really do not know where I belong in this world."

"I understand." A wave of warmth and connection washed through Keiran as he reached for Rosalyn's hand. When she did not pull away, he wrapped his larger fingers around her smaller ones.

Diamonds were created under great pressure. The young woman before him was a diamond in the making—of that he was certain. "I have felt the same need to hide my true self from my family. That is why I am afraid to tell them about my inability to read and write. They will judge me, and treat me like the child they remember, not the man I have become in their absence."

"What do you mean 'child'?" she asked, her expression puzzled.

Rosalyn had asked earlier for answers about her wound and how he had healed her. Perhaps it was time to tell her the truth. "I have only just returned to my family after nine years of being away."

She frowned. "If you were not away at school, then

where were you?"

"I was kidnapped as an infant and taken to Fairyland."

Rosalyn moved to pull her hand from his, but he held fast. "Truly, such a place does not exist."

"I assure you it does. The fairy king adopted me as his own son and gifted me with the power to heal, mostly as a self-protective measure since I was prone to injuring myself."

Her eyes went wide, and her other hand drifted to her abdomen. "I did not imagine . . . You did heal me." Her voice held a sense of awe.

Keiran nodded. "A gift I was grateful to have when I came upon the ambush where you almost lost your life."

"I am certain I died that day. And you brought me back." She held tightly to his hand, as if he were a lifeline. "I imagine growing up in a strange place was difficult for you."

He offered her a wry smile. "Everyone bears scars from the lives they lead. Yet every scar tells a story. Our stories proclaim that we survived. We are here at this moment, together, to either remain stuck in our pain or move ahead towards something better."

A smile came to her lips. "I want to move ahead and be free of men controlling my life."

Keiran nodded. "Geordie Buchannan will help you be free of the contract that binds you to another. Though we both need to heal the injured parts of ourselves by accepting them." He met her gaze. "You are Scottish, but also English. That makes you uniquely you. And I lost fourteen years of my life when Oberon aged me. I am both child and adult in the same body, but I choose to be the adult."

"The fairy king aged you?"

Instead of the pain the thought usually brought, Keiran felt stronger, more resilient. "He did."

She squeezed his hand lightly. "Then I am glad of it so that you are the person before me now." Hope shone in her eyes. "I can help you learn the things you missed."

"And I can help you know what it means to be Scottish, and help myself in the process, for I know only what my brothers have told me about being a Scot." At her gentle smile, Keiran felt as though a weight had been lifted from his chest.

Rosalyn released his hand with another light squeeze, then stood and moved to the bookshelf and retrieved a leather-bound book with gold lettering on the spine. "Let us not wait until tomorrow for me to start your lessons. Let us begin now." She moved towards the door.

Keiran stood and followed her. As they left the chamber, he realised the hurts of their past had made them better equipped to face the present. He only hoped that either Oberon or her betrothed would not swoop in and destroy their tentative friendship and these moments of peace. "Do you like animals?"

Rosalyn frowned as they moved down the hallway, then down the front stairs. "If you mean wild animals who would eat or maim me, nay. If you mean smaller animals like birds or puppies, then aye."

"Then you will like where we are going to study. Come, follow me."

CHAPTER ELEVEN

ROSALYN AND KEIRAN exited the castle through the back door and entered the rear courtyard. Rosalyn smiled at the memory of the lessons she'd had there with the other women this morning. What would Keiran think if she told him she'd learned how to fight and defend herself with the dagger that was now strapped to her thigh in the same manner Aria wore her own weapon?

It was probably best to keep that information to herself for now, but wearing the weapon and having the knowledge to use it bolstered her confidence. She was no longer defenceless. Though she doubted she would need protection from Keiran, even as she wondered where he was taking her. "Where are we going?" she asked as they headed for a brick building near the kitchen.

"The mews."

"Is that not where you keep falcons and other raptors?"

"Among other things since my return." Keiran opened the door then stepped aside for her to enter.

Afternoon light passed through the slatted windows, illuminating the stone interior of the chamber. In one corner of the chamber was a barren tree branch upon which sat not raptors, but a long-eared owl with a bandage around one of its feet. Beneath the perch was a pile of hay on which rested a brown rabbit with a bandage around its middle. Keiran moved to the rabbit and bent down, allowing it to nuzzle his fingers.

Rosalyn watched as he moved about the chamber, feeding the animals. He offered bits of sliced apple and carrots for the rabbits, grain for the smaller birds, and a small fish for the owl before moving to a mother cat curled in the corner of the chamber beneath a small table with two chairs.

"'Tis all right, Midnight," he cooed to the black and white mother cat nursing one tiny kitten. "I simply want to see how you and your babe are doing after such a challenging delivery. The wee one looks healthy, as do you, milady."

"What do you mean 'after a challenging delivery'?" Rosalyn asked, kneeling beside him to look at the two cats.

"I found this mama cat at midnight three days ago in a rainstorm. She was labouring hard and had delivered two stillborn babes before I found her and brought her here." Keiran reached out and gently stroked the white streak running up the kitten's nose. A loud purring sound filled the air. "I was able to help her deliver this wee one, and then I healed the mama cat before she bled out."

Keiran turned to her and smiled broadly, his eyes alive with joy. The lines and furrows of the worry she had seen on his face since yesterday were now completely gone. She met his smile with her own. "It is unusual for men to bring life to the world."

"Aye, men are usually the ones taking life."

"Yet you save life." Rosalyn sat back on her heels as her hand moved to her abdomen. "You heal animals and humans."

"I help those who will accept my healing."

"I would like to help you take care of these animals, if I might," she said, expecting him to dismiss her as her brother always had. Instead, he nodded.

"We can care for them, together."

She had not experienced a "together" moment with anyone since her mother died. It had been Rosalyn alone against the world, for seven long years. Her brother had frightened away any friends she tried to make or any connections she had sought. She had not one loyal friend, even within the household staff. They were too frightened of her brother's wrath. The thought of Keiran as a friend sent a quiver of nervous energy through her.

Only yesterday this man had been her enemy, a fierce warrior. He was also the man who had restored her life and who saved kittens. Which man was the real Keiran? Did she want to find out? "What did you name the kitten?"

He turned back to look at the small creature. "I will leave that up to you. The kitten is yours if you want her."

"I will have to think on that," she replied. Was he asking her to take the kitten with her when she left, or was he asking her to stay? If she named the tiny beast, it would be a commitment on her part. But a commitment to what?

Keiran moved out from beneath the table, close to her, making her heart flutter. She scooted back to allow him to stand. He reached out his hand to aid her in rising. At his nearness Rosalyn lowered her gaze. Keiran was completely at ease standing among the straw, caring for the lives he had saved. Including hers. "What you do here is a miracle. You said the fairies gave you your gift. How does it work exactly? Is it magic or something more?" she asked, curious about what he had done not only to her but also these animals.

"Take a seat."

She did as he directed and put the book she'd brought with her on the table between them. He sat opposite her, leaning his arms on the table and steepling his hands, as if in prayer, before he reached out to turn his palms up. "Place your hands palm down on mine."

She hesitated a moment before doing as he directed. His hands were warm compared to her colder ones. He did not try to capture her fingers. He simply allowed her to rest her palms on his. She studied him in the dim light, trying to read his intentions. What would she find if she could delve into his mind? Was the desire to kiss her as strong as hers was to kiss him? She startled at the thought. The last time she had kissed someone it had cost her nothing but heartache, humiliation, and pain.

Instead of tensing and pulling away, she found herself

leaning forward as the heat of his hands intensified and flowed into her body. The sensation was calming, comforting. This was magic, no matter what he claimed.

"I do not know how my gift of healing works exactly. Over the years I have found that if I touch an injured area, it responds to the warmth. The first time I used my healing powers in Fairyland, I had broken my leg while trying to keep up with the other fairies. Left alone in the mud, I straightened my leg and put both my hands on the broken bones. Immediately the pain left, and I could feel my body knitting itself back together, until I was able to stand and run again."

"That is what I felt when you healed me. At first there was intense pain, and I felt my strength and my life force leaving my body. Then you touched me, a spark flared, and the pain vanished. I drew a breath, filling my lungs, and warmth invaded every part of me. The same warmth as I feel now." She frowned as the heat intensified. "Do you pass this warmth on to everything you touch?"

"Nay." He met her curious gaze. "Only things that need healing."

She jerked her hands from his. Her breath stilled. She was not injured, not physically at least. "Enough of this." She reached for the book. "We are here to teach you how to read."

His brows came together as he looked at the thick tome in her hands. "Should we not start with something a little less intimidating?"

As the residual heat from her hands vanished, her thoughts cleared. "It is better to start with something interesting so you will want to keep reading. I was hoping you would find *Travels into Several Remote Nations of the World. In Four Parts. By Lemuel Gulliver, First a Surgeon, and then a Captain of Several Ships* by Jonathan Swift interesting. It is the story of a man who travels to fantastical lands. It is full of satire and interesting characters. My brother has this book in his library, and I have secretly read it at least three times."

Keiran's brow cleared and interest brightened his eyes. "Your brother does not allow you to read his books?"

"He would prefer I do nothing but embroider his handkerchiefs with the letters HD."

"You like embroidery, then?"

She rolled her eyes, making his mouth pull up in a grin. "No. I hate it."

He raised an eyebrow. "Then let us read this forbidden book and enjoy every moment of these interesting characters in fantastical lands."

She could not help but smile. "Here, you look at the book while I prepare the classroom. You will need to know the letters and what they sound like before you can start reading." She stood. "First, I need to find something with which I can write on these stone walls. I will be better prepared tomorrow when we meet at sunrise, but for now, this will do."

He opened his sporran and handed her a piece of flint. "This should work."

She accepted the flint, moved to the wall opposite the door, and began to scratch the letters of the alphabet onto the stone. Instead of looking at the book, Keiran watched her write each letter, so she named each as she progressed. After she said the letter, he repeated it. As he did, she noted the soft burr in his tone. A tone that was warm and inviting, reminding her of the kitten purring as Keiran had stroked its nose.

She wrote another letter then turned and spoke it aloud. "T," he responded, his lips firm. The throaty sound warmed her almost as much as his hands.

She turned away, inhaling. She was supposed to be teaching him, not losing herself in the nuances of the attractive man before her. Rosalyn hurried through the remainder of the alphabet, and when she had finished, she asked him to start over from the beginning, this time without her aid. He did not miss a single letter. "You are a very quick study."

His lips turned up in a smile. The effect was devastating. His features brightened, his eyes warmed, and against her will, her heart fluttered again.

Rosalyn cleared her throat and turned her attention to the book on the table. "Let us look at the words in here and try to pronounce them so you can see the correlation between letters and words. *Chapter One. My father had a small estate in Nottinghamshire; I was the third of five sons.*" And so, the book continued, introducing Lemuel Gulliver, and setting the stage for his adventurous life as a sea captain. She had had to help him with most of the words, but by the end of the chapter, he was starting to recognise most of the two- and three-letter words on his own.

She shut the book. "That is remarkable progress for your first lesson, Keiran." His advancement was due more to his ability to learn than her own teaching skills, but today he had given her a different gift than his healing. He had given her back a glimmer of hope that her life might amount to something as a tutor.

Instead of the smile she expected at her praise, Keiran shrugged. "I had to learn quickly in Fairyland. It was either learn and survive or fail and die."

Rosalyn flinched. "It is hard to imagine the uncertainty and danger you faced. How did you escape?"

"Aria and Graeme came for me." His brows lowered as he regarded her. "I believe you had similar experiences."

"I was ignored, lonely, but never in physical danger, at least not that I knew about until coming to Scotland."

"Enough about the past." He stood. "Now it is my turn to teach you something about being Scottish. Since you did such a stellar job for our first lesson, my task is made all the harder."

A smile came to her lips. "This is not a competition."

He arched a brow. "It can be if we make it one."

"I understand the benchmark for you. When you can read and write, I will know I have succeeded. How will you know if I have fully embraced my Scottish half or not?"

"I will know and so will you," he said with confidence.

Seemed a little ambiguous but who was she to argue? Her goal could be easily attained. "What about the stakes? I have little left to give."

"You wish to be a tutor, do you not?" Keiran said, his voice gentle.

"It is the only skill I have that might help sustain my life," she said honestly. "After my success with you, I hope to find a permanent position here in the Highlands, for England will never accept me in society again after my misfortune."

"You did not cause your misfortune. The aristocracy would understand that, would they not?"

"The aristocratic ladies will call me a whore and their husbands will try to corner me in empty rooms if I am admitted to any social gatherings," she said tartly. How could he know such a thing, having lived most of his life until now in a fantastical land of his own?

Keiran's gaze turned thoughtful for a moment before his brown eyes held both amusement and a silent plea. "Here is what I propose. If I win our challenge, then you will stay at Dunvegan as a tutor to Alastair and Gwendolyn's children."

She frowned. "Good heavens. They are but infants."

"They will grow, and in the meantime, you could function as their nanny. Gwendolyn does not get much sleep. She could use your help."

"You would want me to stay here?"

He nodded. "Much has happened to us both in our pasts, and I feel a surprising kinship with you."

Since the moment he first took her into his arms to heal her, she had felt the same, but was that reason enough to stay? "And if I win?"

"I will ask Alastair to help find you a position with one of our neighbouring clans, and for myself I would take a kiss."

"One kiss?"

"Aye, but not just any kiss. It must be a meaningful kiss."

She crossed her arms, thinking. With what he offered, she would take a prize if she won or lost this challenge between them. All she had to sacrifice was one kiss. She swallowed roughly. One kiss had led her here to Scotland. Would kissing Keiran lead to a similar disaster? Yet even as the thought took hold it was not fear that sent her heart racing. "I cannot deny your proposal has appeal," Rosalyn said. "We would both be taking a great leap of faith, for we scarcely know each other."

"Or do we know each other better than either of us is willing to admit?" He stared hard into her eyes. "Do you accept?"

She uncrossed her arms. "I accept."

He smiled and gestured to the door. "Then let us go

back to the keep so that I may start you on your journey to becoming a Scot and find my own Scottish roots along the way."

"I can be a formidable opponent," she said.

His smile grew. "I would expect nothing less from you."

CHAPTER TWELVE

THE SUN WAS beginning to set when Rosalyn and Keiran walked in silence back into the castle and headed up the stairs towards the great hall. The only sound along the stone hallway was their footsteps—his firm and regulated as he adjusted to her shorter stride. When they approached the doorway, the sound of laughter and the clinking of glasses came to them. Only then did Rosalyn's nerves falter as her steps slowed. Keiran's hand tightened on her elbow, steering her forward.

"Do not worry," he said with a soft smile. "We MacLeods are a friendly bunch, and rarely if ever sacrifice our guests at the supper table."

She knew his humour was an attempt to put her at ease, and she was grateful for it. "That is well. I was worried about the outcome of this meal with your family." She allowed a small smile to come to her lips. She was not certain why she was so nervous, the MacLeods had been nothing but kind to her since her arrival. Which was very different from the reception she usually received while dining amongst the aristocracy in England.

She and Keiran entered a room full of glittering candle-light and splashes of brightly hued tartan. At their appearance, all conversation ground to a halt and heads swivelled and stared at the two of them in the doorway. Rosalyn felt heat rise to her cheeks, growing warmer as she imagined most eyes were on her, not because she was a visitor but because she was English.

Alastair and Gwendolyn stood and came to the door. "We are so happy that you will join us for supper tonight." Gwendolyn offered her a welcoming smile, then took Rosalyn's arm, and led her to the table on the dais at the front of the room. A cheery fire crackled in the hearth along the far wall, adding warmth to the chamber. "Sit here." She motioned to the chair next to her own.

Keiran appeared beside her and pulled the chair out for her to sit, then took the seat next to her. "If we are both to learn about all things Scottish, then I had best remain close."

Looking around the chamber, Rosalyn noted that the family sat on the dais while the warriors and their families sat at long tables clustered near them. All the men, including Keiran and his brothers, wore green and blue tartan. The women on the dais were elegantly gowned in silks and brocades that were the height of fashion even in England. She had always assumed that the women here were still stuck in the past when it came to fashion. Obviously, she had been very wrong in that regard.

"We hope we did not keep you waiting," Keiran said to

his brothers, lifting his glass of claret to his lips and taking a sip.

Alastair's gaze passed between Rosalyn and Keiran. "We sent Graeme and Callum out looking for you about an hour ago, but they could not find you. Where were you two?" Alastair did not wait for an answer as he signalled the maids waiting against the wall to begin serving the meal.

"Rosalyn and I were exploring the estate. Our path must have just been opposite of Graeme and Callum's." The falsehood seemed to satisfy Alastair.

The maids carried platters of savoury-smelling meats to each table already laden with crisp potato scones browned in bacon fat, as well as fruit, cheese, and bottles of claret. Tender pink salmon on a bed of leeks was followed by sausages, and crispy pasty stuffed with ground venison. All those dishes were unfamiliar to her, but she enjoyed them greatly. Then came the roasted mutton and onions, scents that reminded Rosalyn of home and should have brought her comfort. Instead, her stomach tightened as the meal progressed.

She looked at those gathered around the table, as the realisation of how much she missed eating with others came upon her. Meals at home were often a solitary affair since her brother was always gone, dining with friends, or at engagements to which she had not been invited.

As the meal progressed, Keiran made certain that her wine glass was always full. And by the time she had sampled everything, she was grateful that Highland dress did not involve wearing a tight corset.

"So, you like our Highland victuals?" Keiran asked as he pushed his own plate away.

Rosalyn took a sip of her wine before answering. "I must admit that Highland food has a lot more flavour than English fare. It seems our cook can make but one sauce and pours it on everything."

He laughed. "Mrs Honey, our cook, will be pleased to hear that you enjoyed your meal." He pushed his chair away from the table, stood, then offered her his hand. "Our meals are usually followed by some kind of entertainment. Do you dance, my lady?"

There was a sound of laughter in his voice, and the way the words "my lady" were spoken with his soft brogue sent a shiver of excitement through her. She took his hand and allowed him to lead her into the centre of the room as the tables were pushed back and spirited strains of music sounded over the conversations and noise.

Keiran grasped Rosalyn's hand and pulled her into a type of country dance with a forming circle, but the others thought differently and thrust them into the centre of the ring. Rosalyn held onto Keiran's hands as he twirled her about. Laughter bubbled up in her throat, and she felt almost too breathless to release it. She could not remember the last time she had felt such unbridled joy.

Tonight might be just any other night to the MacLeods

with their delicious food, flowing wine, and dancing, but to Rosalyn it was special. These people were not her family, though that did not seem to matter. She had nothing to offer them, and still they treated her better than her own English relations had over the past few years.

"What are you thinking?" Keiran asked, his steps slowing.

She could not keep a smile from her lips. "That I have had more fun tonight than I have had in a very long time."

"Are you ready to embrace being a Scot?" he challenged.

"I am not," she countered.

"Then perhaps you had better come with me for the remainder of this evening's entertainment. My brothers made certain I knew how to dance when I returned, even though we danced often in Fairyland. But what comes next might be a bit of a surprise as it was to me." He pulled her with him towards the ring of dancers, and they ducked under Alastair and Gwendolyn's raised hands. He did not explain what would happen next as he hurried along the hallway and down the stairs, still holding her hand tight.

At the rear door, he released her as he lifted a green and blue tartan shawl off a hook behind the door and set it about her shoulders. "You will need this. Stay here. I will be right back."

He left her standing there as he disappeared into a chamber on the right. A few seconds later, he emerged with a brown bottle and two glasses. "Come with me," he said as he moved past her and out the door, heading for the rear courtyard. Instead of heading for the mews as she expected, he led her down a path towards a sea gate. He opened it and let her pass and joined her before closing it again.

Since they had last been outside, the sun had set. Night had descended upon the loch like a velvet shroud punctuated only by the twinkling tapestry of the stars above. A sliver of moon hung high in the sky, bathing the shoreline in a silver glow.

Keiran offered her his arm as they made their way across the ragged rocks, until they reached more even terrain where he led her to a large boulder. He set the bottle and glasses down and before she could object, his hands came about her waist as he lifted her onto the rock. A moment later, he joined her and handed her one of the glasses.

"What is this?" she asked as he poured the liquid into her glass, the sound mimicking the waves as they quietly lapped at the shoreline not far from their feet.

"This is *uisge beatha*, which is Gaelic for the water of life," he replied as he poured himself a splash, then set the bottle aside. He raised his glass in a toast. "To being Scottish." He tossed down the liquor in a single swallow.

She pressed her lips together as she sniffed the contents of her glass. "This does not smell like water."

"Because it is whisky." He laughed. "Every good Scot knows how to distil grain, water, and yeast into this essential drink. Even when fairies come to the human realm, they try to leave with a bottle or two to savour back home, though I was never given any until my return two weeks ago."

Rosalyn lifted the glass to her lips, and instead of throwing back the contents, she took a small sip. The initial taste was smoky and earthy on her tongue, but when the liquid hit her throat, it felt more like a fireball had plunged down her throat and temporarily sucked all the air from her lungs.

When she could draw a breath and the sensation returned to her tongue and mouth she choked out, "This must take some getting used to."

Keiran laughed again, but the sound was cut off by what sounded like the screams of a tortured animal.

"What is that sound? I heard it last night but could not identify it." Rosalyn shifted in the direction of the sound. By the time she located a man atop the tallest tower of the castle, the raw screeching had turned to a clean and distinct wailing that sounded more like music.

"Every night following supper, a piper appears on the Fairy Tower to signal the close of the day. He plays the fairy lullaby that was sung by the fairy princess, who centuries ago married Iain Cair MacLeod and was forced by Oberon to leave her child behind. When the child cried, the fairy princess swaddled him in what we now call the Fairy Flag and sang him this song."

"Your family has many connections to Fairyland, doesn't it? The Fairy Flag, Aria, and you."

Even in the darkness she could see him nod. "I suppose

that is why I was stolen from my family—to keep those connections alive even centuries later."

"No matter how much it hurts the MacLeods," she said as the sound of the bagpiper faded away, leaving a heavy silence.

Keiran set his glass aside and leaned back against the rock, staring up at the night sky. "Do you find it strange that both of us have family and yet we have lived much of our lives alone? You have been with family longer than you've been without, and I have been without longer than I have been with my family, yet we are in the same place."

Rosalyn nodded more to herself than to him. She knew the feeling of loneliness well. Even in England, surrounded by people, she had often felt an emptiness that bordered on panic. She risked a glance sideways only to find Keiran looking at her and not the night sky.

"I should have said this before . . . I am sorry about what happened to you with your betrothed."

Rosalyn stared down into her tankard. "You have nothing to be sorry about. Lieutenant Long might have been my betrothed when I came to Scotland, but as far as I am concerned, whether the courts approve my petition or not, that relationship is now severed." Unsettled by her own thoughts, she quickly raised her tankard to her lips and quickly tossed back the contents, hoping it would help her forget about the man who'd tried to kill her.

When the fire in her throat eased, she set her own tankard down and leaned back against the rock, gazing at the stars overhead. It did not take long for the warmth of the whisky to flow through her blood, dulling her senses. "Though I am not quite ready to declare myself a Scot, I must admit that I have had more fun tonight with you than any night I can ever remember."

She could not see, but she sensed his smile in the darkness. Silence once again fell between them. They reclined there, staring up at the night sky as two companions might. Keiran's presence was welcome, even comforting if she were honest. She'd had little time for comfort and friendship in her life, and she had found both this day amongst the MacLeods.

Rosalyn tried to read Keiran's features for some clue about his emotions, but his face was wrapped in a veil of moonlight and shadow. She had only known this man for two days and yet she had never been happier.

He shifted beside her, and for a moment she tensed, fearing he was preparing to leave. Not wanting him to slip away she tried to think of something to say, anything to keep him here, just the two of them, side by side. When he settled back against the rock, putting his hands behind his head, she breathed a sigh of relief.

"Can I ask you something?" she finally said, as the whisky dulled her senses even more.

"Anything," he replied, turning his head towards her.

"If you had the power to change one thing, what would

that be?" The moment she asked the question, she longed to take it back. How many times had her brother reprimanded her for being a dreamer?

"I am certain you wish to hear me say that I had never been stolen by the fairies. But that is not what I would wish because if I had not, the two of us would not be here right now, and you would be dead. Because of that, I feel a sense of obligation to protect you from further harm."

Her chest tightened as she sat up. "You are not responsible for my safety or well-being."

He sat up and turned to her. "I was born a warrior, Rosalyn. In Fairyland and here in the human realm, I was never able to turn away from that part of myself. In Fairyland, I protected the people who had wronged me with just as much ferocity as I protect my family now, and that includes you." He took her hand and laced his fingers with hers. "I cannot deny that I feel responsible for you. Though I do not own you. You are your own person and can decide your own fate."

He reached for her with his free hand and drew her head down to his shoulder until her hair rested against the warmth of his plaid draped across to his left arm. "I would like to help you bear your burdens for a while, Rosalyn. Together we can figure out how your life can move forward."

"I was always taught that I had to figure things out on my own, to survive on my own, with no help from anyone," she said, her voice tight.

"Whether you like it or not you are part of the MacLeod clan now. All of us are here to help you."

"You all have been nothing but kind to me despite who I am." Rosalyn stared down at their intertwined fingers and tried to ignore the comforting thrill of his touch.

He gently rested his chin against the top of her head. "Do you not see that we have a mutual enemy? It is only a matter of time before the English attack the Scots and try to change our way of life here in the Highlands. Lieutenant James Long is as much a threat to us as he is to you."

Giving in to the moment, Rosalyn brushed her thumb against the top of Keiran's hand. Then realising what she had done, she shifted her gaze from their joined hands to the moonlight shimmering on the water of the loch. "If I could change one thing about my life it would be that I had been born male. Then I would not be in this situation at all."

He chuckled, the sound deep and rich. "I, for one, am glad you are not male." He reached up and removed the pin that secured his tartan at his shoulder. A moment later, he pulled her more closely against him, then spread the tail of the fabric across their legs and bodies, enveloping them both in a cocoon of warmth against the encroaching night. "Tell me about your past," he asked in a sincere tone. "You know about my past in Fairyland, I would like to know more about you."

"It is not an extraordinary tale. You know about my parents, but what you do not know is that my father's parents never accepted my mother as his wife. They went out of their way to make life difficult for her in London society. My father never seemed to notice. His love for my mother overshadowed everything. When my brother and I came along, our grandparents were not cruel to us, but they never accepted us." Rosalyn's hand involuntarily tightened on Keiran's. "My mother died one morning when she was taking a carriage to the market. She thought she might be pregnant with her third child and wanted to prepare a few things." Rosalyn swallowed roughly. "I have no proof, but I always suspected that my grandparents had something to do with her accident, as the fasteners on the carriage wheels had been loosened."

Rosalyn closed her eyes as the aching memories swelled inside her. "My father was devastated. He never recovered from her loss. He had nothing to do with Hugh or myself from the time of her death, until he himself passed from a broken heart."

In the silvery darkness Keiran raised his head and searched her face. "How old were you?"

"My brother had only just reached his majority, and I was only twelve."

"That must have been terribly hard for both of you. Did your grandparents help you at all?"

"No. My brother somehow figured out how to move forward with our father's estate and as the new Lord of Thomond. I was only an obstacle in his way. He made it clear from the very first day that he could not wait for me to grow up so that he might be rid of me."

"Which is why he sent you to Scotland."

She was stunned into meekness by the warm and sensual look in his eyes. The rest of the story about her own poor choices would remain her secret.

Keiran's arms tightened around her. "Your brother might not have protected you, but I will. You asked the one thing I would change if I could. It would be that I was betrothed to you and not Lieutenant Long."

"Be serious," Rosalyn said, keeping her voice light despite the sudden tension that tightened her chest.

Keiran leaned even closer, so only fragments of his features were clear to her in the silver moonlight. "I am being serious."

The sincerity of his voice snatched her breath away. She could not allow herself to fall into that trap again. She pulled her hands from his. "Men only say such things to further their own goals."

"I am not like most men. You know that. Even in the two days we have been together, you sensed that I am different." He took her chin between his thumb and forefinger and lifted it, forcing her to meet his steady gaze. He was close enough for her to see him clearly in the moonlight. "I am sincere in my determination to protect you. Please hear me out before you turn against my idea."

She had no choice but to stare into the dark intensity of

his gaze. She saw no deception there, only an earnest desire for her to listen. "You have been poorly treated by the men in your life. And I can understand your hesitancy to put yourself in a situation where yet another man has control over your life. But I do not want to control you. You are perfect the way you are—strong, brave, and determined. I respect that."

Rosalyn swallowed roughly. No one had ever said such things to her before.

"My desire to protect you is not born of obligation. It is because since the moment I first saw you in the woods, I have not been the same. Your desperate situation brought something deep inside me back to life, something that I kept hidden all the time I was away from my family."

He looked away briefly before returning his gaze to hers. "I have held myself apart from anyone, both fairy and human, for so many years that it became habit. And if I am honest, it was a way to keep from being hurt."

She frowned. "I do not understand. What are you saying?"

"I have as much to lose as you do with what I am about to ask. Lieutenant James Long does not deserve you. The one way we can keep him from hurting you is for you to bind yourself to me. Handfast with me for a year and a day. A secondary, even though it is temporary, commitment to another would have to be resolved in the courts and would keep you from having to honour any prior obligations."

"What if a child comes from such a union?" she asked, needing clarification and a moment to absorb what he asked.

"Then I would care for you both whether you stayed with me or not."

Her frown deepened. "Why would you want to sacrifice yourself like that for me and any possible child?" He released her chin, and she mourned the loss of his warmth. Even so she leaned back, putting some distance between the two of them.

"Because that is what warriors do—we sacrifice ourselves for others. And if I saved your life, it is up to me to protect that life. If the courts do not approve your disillusion of betrothal, the man who tried to kill you may succeed next time."

Rosalyn's body began to tremble. He did not speak of love, only obligation and sacrifice. But what he proposed had merit in that it would keep her safe, for as he said a year and a day. It would also mean putting his life on hold. Could she ask that of him? "Might I have time to consider your offer?"

"That you would consider my offer and not reject it out of hand gives me hope." He smiled as he gathered up the tail of his tartan and secured it at his shoulder once more. "As for tonight, did the food, the dancing, or feeling connected to the land around you convince you in any way to claim your own Scottish heritage as it did me?"

Her thoughts were still a tangled mass of confusion from what he had proposed. Even so she managed to smile. "I need more time for that as well." He had no idea how close she had come to claiming that part of herself this evening when she had been dancing with him. Yet now, here in the open air, sanity had pulled her back to her more cautious self. She needed more time to think not only about his proposal, but about what would be best for her heart. For she was certain if she gave herself to Keiran, even for a year and a day, that she would never be able to move forward without him. She was very much like her father in that respect. Once she gave her heart, it would be forever. But did he even want her heart? Was forever what he offered her, or only a temporary solution to her troubles?

CHAPTER THIRTEEN

F OR THE NEXT three days, Keiran and Rosalyn met at sunrise to continue his lessons. Not only was he starting to read all about Gulliver and his travels, with her assistance, but Keiran had also learned to write his name, and the names of the members of his family, Dunvegan Castle, Dunvegan village, and all the surrounding towns nearby. If Alastair presented him with the map Keiran had acquired from the Nicolsons again, he would now be able to read it. That thought brought a renewed sense of purpose to his soul.

At mid-afternoon every day, Rosalyn disappeared with all the other women of the family for an hour or two, then when she returned, she and Keiran spent the rest of the day either learning about Scotland's history, all the things the Scots had invented, or with him trying to convince her to embrace her Scottish half with food, music, walks along the shores of the loch, or teaching her about her mother's clan.

Today, he and Rosalyn would break their usual pattern because he had something different in mind. He had sent a note to her chamber for her to meet him in the front court-yard after she broke her fast.

He'd had her brown and white horse, Petunia, saddled as well as one of Alastair's dappled grey Andalusians. The breed was not only strong and steady, but courageous in the heat of battle. Not that Keiran expected trouble on their journey today, but it was best to be prepared. Aria and Graeme sat atop their own horses near the gate, ready to accompany him and Rosalyn. Alastair would not agree to Keiran leaving the safety of the castle any other way.

They did not have to wait long for Rosalyn to emerge from the keep. "What is all this?" she asked, coming over to Petunia and reaching up to scratch behind her ears. The mare whuffled at her, then gave her a friendly headbutt. Rosalyn laughed. "She seems to be adjusting very well to the Dunvegan stables. Your stableboys should be commended."

"I will inform them of your praise," Keiran said, moving to Rosalyn's side. He placed his hands to help her up. She set her booted left foot in his hands, and he tossed her up into the saddle. She landed as gracefully as thistledown. She grinned down at him as she adjusted her full skirts to fall over her legs. Bathed in the morning sun, Rosalyn looked enchanting atop her white horse in her new dark green riding habit. It was a perfect foil for her creamy complexion with a light smattering of freckles across her nose and cheeks, brown hair, and hazel eyes.

Keiran moved to his horse, checked the tack, then mounted. In the distance, Graeme signalled for the gate to open. Before they set into motion, a familiar mist gathered in the courtyard as the Grey Lady took form. She remained at a distance, but even so the animals skittered and pranced.

"Good morning, Mother," Keiran said, trying to keep his horse calm. Rosalyn had already soothed Petunia now standing at attention, watching the mist instead of reacting to it.

Before you leave, I had to see you and to warn you that I have had an odd feeling since dawn. I fear if the four of you leave the castle's protection today something terrible might happen.

"All will be well, Mother," Keiran assured her as warmth blossomed in his chest. He had never had anyone worry about him before. "We are taking precautions to keep ourselves safe by travelling on the open roads. Three of us are well armed and are perfectly able to protect ourselves. Though if it will make you feel more comfortable, we will stay close to Dunvegan and if we encounter trouble, we will return immediately."

Lady Janet smiled. *Forgive your mother for being overly cautious. You have only just returned to me, and I do not wish to lose you again.*

Despite her fear, she would allow him to go, a bittersweet expression of her unconditional love. Keiran returned her smile as the warmth in his chest became a tightness. Every day he discovered new things about his family and himself that he had truly missed over the last nine years. "All will be well, Mother. We will return shortly. And when we do, we will call you forth so that you may see we are unharmed."

Keiran turned and headed for the gate. Rosalyn followed as their horses still pranced with residual fear, but once they were clear of the gate they settled into a regular gait.

"We will travel to the north-east, along the coastline that is open and clear of brush as I promised my mother. The clear path will be good for a gallop when you are ready."

"I am ready." She set off at a canter in the direction he indicated.

By the time they were on the trail, she and her mare were flying. He kept pace behind her, enjoying the speed and watching her ride. He had no idea she was such a talented horsewoman. Eventually, she slowed her mount to a trot as the trail turned to the north.

She twisted to look at him, her face flushed with pleasure. "It feels wonderful to be out in the open. I have not felt such freedom in a very long while." As he came alongside her, she asked, "Where are we going?"

"To a place where you can feel your Scottish roots more fully. I have never been there, but Alastair assured me it is a magical place where anyone with Scottish roots can become one with the land and the sea."

"Then I am excited to see this place. I must admit Scotland and her people are starting to work their way into my heart," she said, turning back to the path ahead, hiding her face from him.

Even so, Keiran latched on to her words as a thread of

hope that he might win the competition they had agreed upon. Was he more excited that she might stay at Dunvegan, or that he might win a kiss from Rosalyn?

As DAWN TURNED into morning, Lieutenant James Long paced restlessly outside his tent. He had been waiting three days for the two noddies he had sent to Dunvegan Castle to return with information about his betrothed. With every step, the lieutenant knew with more certainty that his men were not coming back. But did that mean they were captured, or had they seen an opportunity to escape him and his regiment and taken it?

The lieutenant drew his sword, displacing a whisper of air as it cut through his disappointment and his growing anger. In all the battles he had fought abroad and here in this godforsaken land, men had fallen at his feet, feeling the bite of his sword. The MacLeods would be no different. They would be easy prey for his well-armed and finely trained regiment. The trick would be to lure them out of their castle, past the woods surrounding Dunvegan, and into the open where his men excelled in fighting.

The question was, how would he lure the MacLeods out? He couldn't capture one of them and hold them for ransom since they were holed up in their fortress. Perhaps he could do the next best thing and attack the village of Dunvegan, light it on fire, and force the MacLeods to come defend their people.

A smile pulled up one corner of his mouth. If a single MacLeod had saved his betrothed in the woods, then what would the MacLeod clan do when he threatened a whole village of people? With possibilities swirling through his mind, the lieutenant sheathed his sword, then headed for his regiment to inform them they would break camp immediately. The MacLeods could not take his betrothed from him and not feel the bite of his anger.

THE SUN WAS almost at its zenith when Keiran and Rosalyn reached the Fairy Glen. A dramatic scene lay before them with small, grassy hills, craggy rock formations, and ponds in between. Rosalyn had no idea what Fairyland was like, but she imagined it appeared something like the landscape in front of her. "I have never seen anything so beautiful. The land feels infused with magic. Are all areas of Scotland like this?"

"There are other areas that are beautiful, I am certain, but my family tells me the Isle of Skye is the land of our people. The connection to the land is as important to us as is the air we breathe and the blood that flows through our veins. And when I explore, I find their words to be more and more true." He stopped his horse beside hers and instead of looking at the scenery, he watched her. "It could mean all that to you as well, if you let it inside your heart."

Rosalyn swallowed roughly as tenderness flared in his eyes. As heat rose to her cheeks, she was grateful for the soft breeze that brushed against her face and tugged at the loose tendrils of hair that had escaped her plait.

Graeme and Aria must have noted her response because they shifted their horses around hers and Keiran's. "We will go on ahead and find a place to secure the horses," Graeme said before he and Aria proceeded down the hill, leaving Rosalyn and Keiran alone.

Keiran shifted his gaze to the landscape. "When Orrick found out we were coming here, he informed me that these rock formations were created over ten thousand years ago in the last Ice Age. He said they were formed by glacial movements. Yet many of the locals seem to believe that this is where fairies live."

"Do fairies live here?" Rosalyn asked, searching his face.

His features tightened. "Fairyland and the human realm are intertwined. Fairies may live under the mounds we see here, or they may not. It is not always easy to tell."

Rosalyn's grip tightened on her reins, causing her horse to dance closer to Keiran's. "Do you have only bad memories of Fairyland?"

He pressed his lips together and for a moment she thought he would not answer her. "I was under an enchantment while I was there which made everything seem

GERRI RUSSELL

different than it was. When the enchantment ended, I saw the truth. My whole life had been a lie." Pain flared in his eyes. "None of that matters now that I am here. My family loves me. What more could I want?"

"Keiran, neither of us can undo our past." Rosalyn noted the lines of grief and wariness at the corners of his eyes. "Since coming to Dunvegan, you have taught me that it is my past that has made me who I am today. Because of you, I was given a second chance to live. I could have chosen to wallow in the misery that had been my prior life. Instead, I am choosing to live, to embrace each moment, allowing it to make me stronger and more of who I am meant to be."

"You are correct." Weariness vanished from his eyes. "Thank you for that reminder. Today is what is important because who knows what tomorrow might bring." For a moment, his gaze drifted into the distance as though looking for something only he could see. A heartbeat later, he turned back to her. "Shall we go explore?"

At her nod, they found the place Graeme and Aria had left their horses then started off down the hill, leaving their horses to graze near a large rock formation that Keiran called Castle Ewen. "The spire here is not a true castle, only a geological formation that many before us believed was a fairy castle."

Graeme and Aria went to climb the castle, while Keiran led Rosalyn towards a series of large, mystical stone spirals.

She moved to the centre of the stones as she took in the

vastness of the land surrounding her. A sense of awe and humility flowed through her with a growing intensity as she drew in the scents of the earth and the sky. Had her Scottish ancestors visited here? Had they felt the same sense of peace and tranquillity that came over her now? She closed her eyes, breathing slowly, feeling a connection to all living things. When she opened her eyes, Keiran stood before her.

"You feel it, do you not? That you are a small part of something bigger?"

She shivered as her heart began to thunder in her chest. "Is this what you feel? What all Scots feel? A profound connection to nature itself?"

He took her in his arms. "I cannot speak for all my people, but it is what I increasingly feel."

She turned her face up to his. Searching his comforting gaze, she felt an overwhelming sense of peace. He was so close. Close enough to kiss. She shifted forward, bringing her lips close to his.

"Does this mean you feel Scottish? That you concede to our competition?"

"Aye," she said instead of her usual "yes."

His lips brushed hers at first, then his arms closed more tightly around her, pulling her against the firmness of his chest as he kissed her deeply, persuading her to open herself to him as shivers tingled through her limbs.

She inhaled sharply and pulled back to stare into his face. His features were taut with strain but there was also something that had not been there before. Hope and desire.

Her tongue came out to moisten her lips as she tried to form the words to tell him she felt it too—a surge of something light and wonderful and pure. Before she could form the words, his lips descended on hers again. In response, her hands slipped up to his shoulders. Her touch became explorative as her lips softened beneath his. He deepened the kiss, demanding more from her in a world that had gone suddenly rich and sensual.

What was she doing? Rosalyn dragged her mouth from Keiran's and shifted her head down against the frantic beating of his heart. "Your prize has been claimed," she said in a ragged voice, trying to calm her own rapidly beating heart.

He stepped back, arms falling to his sides, his eyes still burning with the same desire she had seen there moments before. "Aye. It has. Yet, I—" His unsaid words hung between them.

Rosalyn wrapped her arms about her waist, fighting the urge to pull him close and lose herself in his kiss once more. She finally understood the desire that had destroyed her parents. Her one brief kiss with Lieutenant Long had caused no such reaction in her. With Keiran, her senses had been bombarded with sensation. The moment his lips had met hers, there had been a bond, a closeness, a sense of delight as well as vulnerability. And for a heartbeat, she had trusted him not to hurt her even though evidence pointed to the fact that was where this kind of connection would lead. "You are the one who wanted a kiss."

He stepped farther away. "Let us go and join Graeme and Aria at the top of the castle formation." He did not wait for her as he headed for the tallest peak in the Fairy Glen.

Rosalyn hesitated as every nerve in her body tingled at the memory of Keiran's kiss, and the thrilling warmth of his body tight against her own. She pressed her hand to her lips, recalling the gentleness of his touch. This kiss had not been rough; it had held a certain reverence, a tenderness that she had not expected. She dropped her hand and took a step when something shimmered in the fairy ring in which she stood. Streaks of white light appeared, widening, and elongating a few steps from her.

She tried to step back, but her feet remained rooted in place. Rosalyn's heart thundered in her chest as she watched the shifting light darken, then take form.

Far away a voice called. "Rosalyn . . ." The words echoed in her mind as a man formed before her. He was tall, with white hair, pale skin, and piercing blue eyes. He wore a golden crown on his head and his clothing was aristocratic yet seemed to be made from the fibres of trees and leaves.

He drew a sword. It flashed in the air. A scream lodged in her throat as the weapon came down. Then, the man vanished, leaving an empty space where he had stood with raised sword only a heartbeat ago. Her body trembled. In the distance, Keiran raced towards her. His steps seemed slow, exaggerated, as her heartbeat filled her ears. Then finally he reached her and wrapped his arms around her. Held her close until the frantic beat of her heart slowed.

"'Tis all right. I will never let him hurt you," Keiran whispered against her ear.

Feeling more settled, Rosalyn pulled back. "Who and what was that? You saw it, did you not? I did not imagine him?"

"I saw him," Keiran said, his voice raw. "Oberon, the fairy king, is alive and trying to return to the human realm."

She concentrated on his words. "Oberon?"

"Aye. And that is not a good thing for any of us. Come." He looped his arm around her waist and led her to the castle formation. When Keiran and Rosalyn approached, they hurried down from the rugged peak. As they came closer, Rosalyn could see the worry in their eyes. Were they afraid for her, or was something else amiss? A knot of fear tightened Rosalyn's stomach.

"What is it?" Keiran asked when the couple reached them, sensing it was not the reappearance of Oberon that drained the colour from their faces.

Graeme met their gazes, but Aria stared into the distance.

"From atop the castle we could see a fire in the north-west near Dunvegan village," Graeme said.

"Was it set by the fairy I saw?" Rosalyn asked, bringing Graeme and Aria's questioning eyes to hers.

The air around them became heavy and still. "Oberon

tried to enter this realm," Keiran said. "He failed, but eventually he will succeed."

"He is definitely alive?" The pitch of Aria's voice rose.

Keiran nodded. "But it appears he is not our only problem at present. Oberon would not have done anything to destroy nature. His targets are always those made by man. So who could have set the fire?"

Graeme frowned. "Any number of our enemies, though I would wager it has something to do with Rosalyn more than the MacLeods." His gaze shifted to her.

Rosalyn's breath caught and she pulled away from Keiran's side. "Lieutenant Long did this?" Guilt and anger over all those who would suffer because of her consumed her. She balled her fists.

"'Tis all right, Rosalyn. Not that a fire is good, but the village is abandoned."

Graeme nodded. "Whoever set that fire most likely did not know all the residents had moved into the castle when we were being attacked by the MacDonalds."

"You believe no one will be hurt?" Rosalyn asked, her fists loosening.

"Fire is destructive." A hint of panic laced Aria's words. "It could spread to the forest where my sister and mother live. We must hurry back and douse the flames."

"We must proceed cautiously." A hand on Aria's arm held her back. "Our enemy might want us to rush to quench the flames, then attack when we are distracted." He turned to Keiran. "You and Rosalyn should return to Dunvegan and gather reinforcements. Aria and I will head to the village and pray that the MacLeod warriors have not responded to the flames and fallen into a trap."

Aria and Graeme moved towards the waiting horses, mounted, then set off towards Dunvegan. Keiran and Rosalyn followed, urging their horses into a run, flying over the open terrain.

Rosalyn could only stare at the black smoke rising in the distance. Even without proof, she knew her once-betrothed was responsible. Her fingers tightened around the reins in her hand. Her chest constricted at the thought that she had brought pain to the MacLeods and their people.

As unshed tears burned the back of her throat, she glanced at Keiran. His bearing was proud, and a look of determination had settled across his brow. Yet she did not miss the lines of worry that were etched beneath his watchful eyes. Their kiss and even Oberon's reappearance seemed far from his thoughts as he concentrated on the billowing flames still so far away.

CHAPTER FOURTEEN

I N THE FOREST, Pearl watched as her fairy-daughter scrambled down from the canopy of the trees as the crackle and hiss of flames devouring the forest around them sounded in the distance.

"Mother, Dunvegan village is burning, and the flames are heading our way!" Panic laced Gille's voice.

Thick smoke filled the air, and the yellow-gold tongues of the flames could be seen, growing stronger as they ravaged everything in their path. The mother-daughter fairies had taken up residence in the forest after their return to the human realm instead of living at Dunvegan with Aria. The forest had felt more like Fairyland, or home, to them both. But their home was now under attack.

Gille came to stand before her mother. "We must do something before the forest is consumed."

Pearl took her daughter's hand, trying to reassure her. "Fear not. I can douse the flames with the nearby stream while you use your magic to create a wall of soil between the forest and the flames. Close your eyes and imagine the soil moving at your command."

Gille scrunched her eyes closed tightly in concentration. A moment passed, then two. And suddenly, the forest floor shifted as a wind rose up, putting an earthen wall between them and the flames.

"Excellent," Pearl acknowledged before she closed her own eyes, raised her hands, and concentrated on moving the water from the nearby stream to the village not far away. The water shifted towards the village in a finely controlled arch then came down softly upon the burning structures. After several long minutes, the flames died down, even as the smoke intensified, causing them both to cough between gasps for breath. Once she was certain the fire had been contained, Pearl motioned for the two of them to head deeper into the forest where the air was less dense with smoke.

Even though the danger had passed, fear lingered in Gille's green eyes. "Something else is wrong, Mother. Something not of this world. I can sense it."

Pearl tensed, knowing what that strange feeling meant. She had felt it too, a familiar presence not of the human realm. "Oberon has returned." They had not sent him to his doom when they had used their magic against him in Fairyland.

"Did he set the fire?" Gille asked.

"Nay," Pearl assured her daughter calmly even though her blood felt thick and hot in her veins and her heartbeat jittered wildly in her chest at the thought of the fairy king emerging once again. "That was the work of human men, and I fear that does not bode well for those who reside at Dunvegan Castle." She turned her gaze to Gille. "We must go to them with all due haste."

SILENCE FELL OVER Aria, Graeme, Keiran, and Rosalyn as they retraced their steps from this morning. It was late afternoon when they reached a rise in the landscape and could see Dunvegan village below. The billowing flames had died and only the acrid scent of burning wood, smoke, and ash drifted through the air.

Yet even through the smoke and ash from the east, they could see clearly the men dressed in the green and blue tartan, heading for the village. And to the east, they could also see several columns of men dressed in red.

"God's teeth," Graeme growled. "Our fellow warriors do not know the English lie in wait." He urged his horse down the rise with Aria close behind.

"Stay here," Keiran ordered, the words harsh, before he drew his sword and chased Graeme and Aria down the hillside. An unfamiliar cry erupted from their throats, an ancient call to arms perhaps, warning those below of impending danger.

Rosalyn's gaze followed Keiran as he headed for the charred remains of the village. She shivered at the thought of what might have happened if the MacLeods had not moved their people to safety. Still, their homes were now ruined because of her and Lieutenant Long.

She released her pent-up breath while Graeme, Aria, and Keiran reached the other MacLeod soldiers in time to warn them of what lay in wait. In that same moment, the sound of horse hoofs came from behind her, and Rosalyn turned atop her horse to see Lieutenant James Long also on horseback, towering over her. A shiver of cold fear moved through her at the hatred darkening the Englishman's face. She'd been taught her whole life to fear the Scots, but it was the man before her who was truly the barbarian.

"My dearest bride, how kind of the MacLeods to leave you alone so I can now claim what is rightfully mine."

"I am not your bride," Rosalyn snapped, holding tight to her horse's reins when the mare quivered beneath her. "You killed that woman days ago."

Lieutenant Long laughed. The sound grated against her taut nerves. "I had nothing to do with your attack. Besides, you look very much alive to me." His mouth quirked into a terrible smile.

"I am alive, no thanks to you, but the woman who was once betrothed to you exists no more." His confused expression helped her to clamp back her emotions.

She straightened in her saddle and said, "My name is Rosalyn Murray, and I am not betrothed to you." Look fear in the face and you will find both courage and strength, Aria had taught her. With her lessons in fighting, Rosalyn was no longer the defenceless girl who had been attacked in the woods. She was so much more.

"Your ploy will not work." The lieutenant brought his horse closer and drew his sword. "I own you. No one else shall have you if I cannot."

"It is no ploy, only the truth." She kept her horse steady, holding her ground. She inhaled a slow, calming breath. The late afternoon sun brought out the lines that had settled around the lieutenant's grey eyes. What she had once thought was his most interesting feature now appeared overly bright and unfocused as those eyes narrowed.

"Are you going to stare at me all day or come with me back to my camp without a fuss?" he asked mockingly.

He should be prepared for more than "a fuss." Rosalyn held Petunia steady as he brought his horse close enough to grab her left wrist. Bring them in close, then fight hard and fast. Remembering Isolde's words, she quickly lifted the hem of her gown, drew her dagger from its sheath, then slashed the lieutenant's upper arm.

Startled, he loosened his grip and she jerked free. With a curse, he brought his sword down. She quickly switched her blade against her forearm and blocked his strike. At the same time, she kicked out, her heel connecting with his gut with all her strength. He roared as he lurched backwards, falling from his saddle, his feet stuck in the stirrups.

He hung there, upside down, roaring in anger. Taking

advantage of his upset, with her heart pounding and her hands shaking, Rosalyn sheathed her dagger and set her horse into motion. The animal needed no further encouragement to race down the hillside.

She was only halfway down before she saw Keiran riding towards her. Fear and anger mixed in the depths of his dark eyes. He joined her then turned his horse back towards the village. When they were just outside the smoking ruins, Keiran stopped his horse, then reached out for her bridle, forcing her to also come to a halt. "He did not hurt you, did he?"

"I hurt him and his pride more than he hurt me." Now that she was at a distance from the lieutenant, she allowed herself a small smile at being able to escape him. "I will have to thank your sisters for giving me lessons in fighting."

Keiran's brows drew together, but when she drew back her skirt to expose not only her thigh, but also her dagger, a smile of appreciation came to his lips. "Is that where you go every day? I will have to thank them myself." He released her bridle as his smile faded. "I only wish you never had to use those skills. I should not have left you alone. As soon as I realised the others were safe, I came back to you."

She looked about her. "Where are the others?"

"Graeme and Aria were able to stop the men from riding into the English regiment's trap. They are all heading back to Dunvegan. I suggest we do the same before our enemy realises they have been foiled."

She nodded, trying to stop her hands from shaking. After all that had happened, she was eager to get back to safety behind the thick stone walls. Both strange and wonderful things had happened since they'd left this morning. She'd almost been attacked by the fairy king. She'd fought off a man who thought he could control her. And she had kissed Keiran. Despite everything inside her that told her it was unwise, she wanted to kiss him again to see if that same trembling, instinctive, and dangerous response raced through her.

That thought stayed with her until they rode over the drawbridge and cleared the open gates of Dunvegan. As soon as they entered the front courtyard, the drawbridge was raised, and the portcullis came down. Many of the warriors remained in the courtyard, preparing their horses to return to the stables, and talking excitedly about how the fire in the village had somehow seemed to extinguish itself.

Ignoring the chaos, Keiran slipped from his horse, then helped her down with his hands at her waist. "If anything had happened to you today, I would never have forgiven myself." He held her close, searching her face. "What did Lieutenant Long say to you?"

"He does not believe that I am no longer the woman he betrothed." She pressed her lips together, thinking, then said, "I cannot explain it exactly, but I sensed he only wanted me because I do not want him."

"There are men like that who want to possess what they

cannot have." Keiran's brows came together.

"And what kind of man are you?" She no longer believed he was the brutal Highlander she had been taught to believe.

"I am a man who wants to protect you from harm, from men like Lieutenant Long. I am the man who wants to handfast with you."

"I can protect myself, Keiran," Rosalyn said, staring up into his eyes.

He drew her closer, despite the presence of the warriors who still roamed the courtyard. "Are you certain of that?" he asked, lifting her hand, and turning it over to expose her wrist. His breath rushed warm and swift against her tender flesh, sending shivers up her arm. "Can you defend yourself against this?"

He pressed his mouth to the inside of her wrist. The sensitive skin heated beneath his lips. She clutched her skirt with her opposite hand, fighting the sensations that threatened to weaken her knees.

He raised his head slightly. "Lieutenant Long is a skilled warrior. You got lucky today because he underestimated you. Believe me, he will not do so again." His pupils flared as his gaze drifted to her mouth, but instead of bringing his lips to hers, he nuzzled her neck, running his chin along her jawbone to the base of her ear. His breath whispered against her ear in a silken caress. "Oberon—he has magic. How will you defend yourself against that with one small dagger?"

As waves of pleasure battered her defences, she released

the hold she had on her dress and instead clamped onto the fabric of his tunic. She shut her eyes, savouring the exotic sensations. "Are you trying to frighten me or seduce me?"

"Perhaps a little of both." Keiran lowered his head and captured her lips. His fingers splayed across her shoulders as his tongue brushed against her lips. She could not deny him the deepest secrets of her mouth or anything else he wanted in that moment. His tongue slipped into her mouth, and she responded by curling her fingers around his nape, drawing him even closer until she realised what she was doing.

She dropped her hand, broke the kiss, and stepped back. Her breathing came in ragged gasps as though she had been racing through the woods instead of the fleeting few moments that had passed in his arms. Kissing him, she was quickly learning, was madness. Even she, who should know better, was finding Keiran hard to resist.

In her continued silence, Keiran released her waist and stepped away, his eyes still burning with the same desire that echoed in her own body. "I want what is best for you, Rosalyn. Joining our lives, however temporarily, will keep Long from claiming you as his own."

"You believe handfasting with you will serve that purpose?" She wanted more than anything to step back into his embrace. It took all her willpower to hold herself back. "You also said that handfasting lasts for a year and a day. What happens after that? We simply go our separate ways?"

Hope crept into his gaze. "If after that time, we decide

we do not suit, we go our separate ways, but we may also decide at any point to seal our bond forever."

The husky sincerity of his voice snatched her breath away. Even so, she could not allow herself to fall into a trap of her own making. She had to make this decision with her head and not her heart. "What if you tire of me before a year? Will you simply put me out of the castle with nowhere to go?"

"If you agree to handfast, then as I assured you before, I would have Mr Buchannan draw up an agreement that guarantees you and any child of mine will be looked after. As Alastair's estate manager, I would receive a generous income. I would give it all to you." He reached for her and once again brought her close to his chest. "As for tiring of you. I never see that happening. The day of your attack, I settled you onto my lap, asking you to stay with me, and brushed my lips against yours." His gaze dropped to her lips. "I have not been the same since. Something passed between us in that moment, something magical."

Then it was not only she who had felt the spark that had danced on her lips when he had kissed her. Rosalyn's entire body began to tremble. His lips descended to hers.

He took her hand and pulled her with him into the shadows of the portico. "We have a bond, you and I," he whispered as he placed feather-light kisses across her chin, then up to her ear.

Rosalyn caught a deep, shuddering breath as he traced a

line of scorching kisses down the sensitive skin of her neck. The warmth of his breath stirred the tendrils of hair that escaped her plait as his mouth began retracing a path back to her lips. One kiss and all thoughts of denying him vanished. By denying him this moment, she would be depriving herself of something almost as vital to her existence as the air she drew into her body, air that mingled with his as they came together in a kiss both poignant and possessive.

He urged her lips to part, and when she did, he delved into her mouth, stroking and caressing, demanding even more of herself than she offered him now. He would consume her body and soul. Could she give him that much of herself and still remain whole? Her father had not been able to continue in this life without her mother, leaving Rosalyn behind to walk a tragic path.

There was so much more to consider than only her own desperate needs. He had promised to take care of her if they found they did not suit, but would she be strong enough to keep moving forward if he did? Yet even as the thought occurred to her, she knew the answer. She was nothing like her father. If she was, she would have given up long ago when things became difficult with her brother.

She had learned, in the intervening years since her parents' deaths, how to survive. Since coming to Scotland, she also realised she possessed inner strength, and was more than capable of picking up the pieces of her life, rebuilding herself, and coming back stronger than ever before. On a shuddering breath, she broke the kiss and pulled back to look into Keiran's passion-glazed eyes. "Yes," she said, her voice tight with emotion. "I will handfast with you for a year and a day."

Keiran bent down and kissed her quickly, then released her almost as abruptly. "Let us cleanse ourselves of our travel dirt, then meet in the rear courtyard at dusk. There, we will pledge ourselves to each other with my family in attendance."

Rosalyn nodded, somewhat disappointed by his response. She did not expect him to whoop for joy in the courtyard still filled with men, but she had hoped for something more demonstrative than a quick kiss on the lips. Though this time, the decision to bind herself to another had been hers, and not her brother's. She would have to find a measure of joy in that thought.

Coming out of the portico, he signalled for one of the stable boys to take their horses, then took her hand in his, leading her into the castle. At the stairs, he stopped. "Until dusk." His voice was suddenly warm and low, and an intensity filled Keiran's expression she had never seen before.

At the sight, she smiled. He was more affected by her agreeing to bind herself to him than he expressed in the open. The thought brought an odd jumble of pleasure and warmth to her chest. "Until dusk," she whispered before hurrying up the stairs to her chamber. Only a few more hours remained until she would bind herself to the man who had given her a second chance at life.

CHAPTER FIFTEEN

ROSALYN STOOD ALONE in her chamber, wondering how a person prepared for handfasting. She knew from a couple of weddings she had attended in London what was involved there, but handfasting was new to her. She moved to the wardrobe and opened it, trying to decide which of her five gowns she would wear.

A knock sounded on the door. "Come in," she said, welcoming the distraction.

Gwendolyn appeared, followed by a man carrying a copper hip bath, and three others carrying pails of steaming water. "Keiran asked to have a bath sent up to you. And I am here to help you prepare for this evening." It was then that Rosalyn noticed the length of tartan in Gwendolyn's hands, along with a bath sheet. She set the items on the bed.

"Place the bath near the fire," Gwendolyn directed the men. As soon as they finished filling the bath, they departed the chamber, closing the door behind them. "Quickly now," Gwendolyn said, coming to help unlace Rosalyn's gown. "Let us remove your riding clothes and get you in that water before it cools. We have plenty of work to do and little time to do it in to prepare you for joining your life to Keiran's."

She paused in working the laces and placed a hand on Rosalyn's arm. "We are all so pleased to have you become a part of our family."

"Only for a short time." Rosalyn swallowed roughly. "We have made no more commitment to each other than that."

Gwendolyn squeezed Rosalyn's arm. "Give it time. You will have lots of that in the next year."

Rosalyn soon found herself in the bath while Gwendolyn gathered garments for Rosalyn to dress in afterwards. It felt good to wash the travel dirt from her skin and hair in the heather-scented water. Weary from travel, she leaned back against the copper tub, wanting to forget about Lieutenant Long and even Oberon. The appearance of the fairy king had seemed to startle Keiran. Was it because the fairy had come into the human realm or was there something more that he had yet to tell her about his time in Fairyland?

As she relaxed, her thoughts turned to Keiran. When she had died on the day they met and she had hovered over her body, God had shown her that he was a good man. But all the years of being told that he was her enemy had made her look for further proof. Over the last six days, he had shown her in so many ways that her first impression of him was correct. Soon, she would bind her life to his, and find either immense happiness or deep sorrow. Only time would reveal that outcome.

"The water has chilled. Come, let us get you dressed," Gwendolyn said, approaching the tub with a bath sheet for Rosalyn to wrap herself in.

After Rosalyn dried herself and her hair, Gwendolyn held out a fresh white chemise with lace at the edge of the sleeves. She slipped it over Rosalyn's head, then set to positioning the stays. When they were in place and tight against her chest and waist, Gwendolyn lifted Rosalyn's hem, handing her a pair of stockings and slippers. "Put these on."

Completing that task, Rosalyn then reached for the sheath that contained her dagger, fastening it at her thigh.

Gwendolyn's eyes went wide. "You will not need that tonight."

Rosalyn frowned. "Isolde said I should keep this on me no matter what." She tightened the fasteners before shifting her skirts down.

Gwendolyn shook her head as she turned to pick up a beautiful dark brown damask dress. "Now, for one of your new gowns." She tossed it over Rosalyn's head. After it floated down to her hips, the young woman tied the gown at the back, cinching Rosalyn's waist.

"You look lovely," Gwendolyn said with a smile. "Now we must do something with your hair." She guided Rosalyn to a chair in front of the fire, then set to brushing out her still-damp hair until it was sufficiently dry. She gathered Rosalyn's hair up high and coiled it into a knot, and secured it with pins, before pulling some curls loose to cascade down

from the top. When she was done, she came around to study Rosalyn and said, "I almost forgot the most important part." She hurried back to the bed and returned with the length of tartan. Encouraging Rosalyn to stand, she fastened the tartan about her waist. "Perfect. Come look at yourself in the polished glass."

Rosalyn moved to the long mirror in the corner of the chamber. The skirts of her dress belled out, making Rosalyn's waist look small. The tight stays lifted her breasts high so that the swell of them breached the neckline of her dress. The tartan that flowed over her hips made her feel somehow connected to the clan she was about to join, however temporarily. "Thank you, Gwendolyn. Please thank your seamstress for me. This gown is simple, yet stunning."

"I would argue that the woman makes the gown stunning, not the other way around. Keiran is a lucky man." Gwendolyn moved to the window and looked outside. "Everyone has gathered in the rear courtyard and the sun is setting. We had best be on our way down."

Gwendolyn walked down the stairs before Rosalyn, looking back over her shoulder with an encouraging smile. As they made their way to the back courtyard, the hum of voices sounded. "We should wait here at the doorway until the piper begins."

Rosalyn reached for Gwendolyn's hand, squeezing it. "I truly appreciate all you have done to help me. I never expected such kindness from anyone after the death of my parents."

Gwendolyn's face softened as she leaned in and kissed Rosalyn's cheek. "I learned from my own unfortunate experiences that where there is life, there is hope. Stay hopeful and trust Keiran, Rosalyn. That is all I ask of you."

Rosalyn felt her throat tighten as she turned her gaze towards those gathered outside. She could see Keiran standing near the crenellated wall with his brothers. Behind him the last rays of the sun lingered on the horizon, staining the loch a golden orange that bled into a dusky rose and smoky plum. Dusk was upon them, a pause before the moon would dominate the night sky. A moment later, the skirl of a bagpipe drifted upon the night air in a seductive serenade.

"'Tis time," Gwendolyn said, leading Rosalyn to the doorway where Keiran had come forward to wait for her.

Her heartbeat thudded wildly at the sight of Keiran, tall and handsome in a fresh white shirt and green and blue tartan with thin lines of yellow and red. At the sight of her, a look of appreciation entered his eyes. He held out his hand and she slipped her trembling right hand into his. The piper's song died down, leaving only the silence of the near-night as Keiran wrapped his strong fingers around her own. Standing so close, she could smell the hint of fresh, clean soap lingering on his skin, and feel the warmth radiating from his nearness.

With his free hand, he reached into his sporran and withdrew a length of red cord. "I wish to bind myself to you,

Rosalyn, for a year and a day." He placed the red cord over their entwined hands.

A shiver moved through Rosalyn at the feel of the cord as Keiran wrapped the length around their joined hands three times. "To keep you safe and protect you from harm."

Even though she bristled at the word "protect", she realised that as a warrior, that was who he was, who he had been born to become in this clan. He would protect her as he did the rest of his family. There was nothing more to his words than that. At her hesitation, a spark of uncertainty entered his gaze. "Will you also pledge yourself to me?"

At that small hint of vulnerability, all her reservations faded. That brief glimpse into his soul reminded her of why they were here in this moment. They were so alike, the two of them. She might have less control over her life as a female than he did as a male. But when the fairies had stolen him from his cradle, he'd also had little control over his life. In the last few days, they had been both working hard to regain what they had lost.

She tightened her hand on his, hoping to say without words that she recognised his sacrifice for her benefit. "I wish to bind myself to you, to be the helpmate you deserve, for a year and a day." Rosalyn stared down at the red cord between them. Red. The colour of courage, strength, and passion. The last thought sent a surge of heat through her body that culminated in her belly.

Standing nearby, Alastair smiled and raised their joined

hands. "With this cord, the two of you have bound your lives into one." Alastair shifted his gaze between the two of them. "Rosalyn and Keiran, with the Lord and these good people as your witnesses, your lives are joined. May the next year find you bound in spirit as you are now bound in life."

When Alastair finished speaking, Keiran drew their joined hands back, and leaning forward, he pressed a kiss, feather-light, across the back of her hand. "I pledge you my life," he said with steely resolve.

His life but not his love. The words brought an ache to Rosalyn's chest. She forced the feeling away. Love was not what this binding was about. It was about protection. She could not deny that she needed his protection. It was comforting to know she would not have to stand alone against whatever Lieutenant Long would bring along with his regiment to Dunvegan eventually.

A cheer rose up from those gathered. A moment later, the skirl of the bagpipe sounded, filling the night air with joy and merriment. The beat of a drum and dulcet tones of Callum on his mandolin joined the piper. Instead of looking at Keiran, Rosalyn kept her gaze on the cord that bound them. "Should we not remove the cord now that the deed is done?"

With a finger beneath her chin, Keiran lifted her gaze to his. A sizzle of heat slipped from his skin to hers. "The cord usually remains in place until our bond is consummated." His smouldering gaze dropped to her lips, and Rosalyn felt her body ignite.

Somewhere in the back of her mind she'd known that was where handfasting would lead. She trusted Keiran, and he trusted her, but was she ready to give herself to him fully? Though her body warmed at his nearness, though her hands longed to reach out and touch him, she held back.

Sensing her hesitation, Keiran released her chin to stroke his finger along her cheek, then curled it in a tendril of her unbound hair. Her body tingled, as if a spark had ignited between them. His touch opened something inside her, a recognition from deep within, that what they had was something special, almost magical. She stared up at him as moonlight shone on his features, giving him an ethereal look that assured her she could trust him with her mind and her body. "Keiran, I—"

A giant sucking sound filled the air. The musicians stopped playing and everyone turned towards the loch and Little Minch beyond. In horror, they watched the water roll back, leaving a huge expanse of empty beach. In the far distance, a huge wave swelled, glittering in the moonlight, appearing like a wall that stretched from the sea to the sky.

"Everyone, inside the castle!" Alastair shouted.

"What is it? What is happening?" Rosalyn asked, fear lacing her voice.

"Go inside." Keiran quickly unwrapped the cord from their hands and set her away from himself. "Go inside. I beg you."

At the fear in his voice, pain tightened Rosalyn's chest. "Does this have something to do with Oberon? The fairy I saw earlier today?"

He nodded. "He means to kill us all. Please, help the others and seek safety inside."

Rosalyn doubted a wave that massive would spare the castle or anyone inside it. A low rumbling built, and the wind swirled around them as those gathered in the courtyard swarmed towards the doorway.

"Please, Rosalyn." His voice was harsh and strained. "I could not bear it if something happened to you."

Startled by the desperation in his words, she hesitated, and noted that Aria and two other cloaked figures remained in the courtyard, their hands outstretched as though fighting the inevitable rush of the water that would consume them all.

"I must help Aria, Pearl, and Gille. The four of us might be able to undo what Oberon has set in motion."

She finally nodded and headed for the doorway that Graeme held open for her. "Hurry," he yelled as the temperature suddenly dropped and a mist appeared between herself and the door.

The mist rose from the ground, then slithered and coiled, releasing a pale light that cut through the silvery darkness.

Rosalyn stopped as her breath quickened, and fear wended though her. The mist grew brighter, like pale snow against

GERRI RUSSELL

a canvas of black, painting the silhouette of a masculine form
where there had once been nothing. The form swirled,
becoming a twisting, dancing light before solidifying into the
being she had seen in the fairy circle earlier today. Fear rose
up inside her as his startling blue gaze connected with hers
and then Keiran's.

Keiran kept his gaze fixed on the fairy king. "What do
you want?"

"What do I want? Where should I begin?" Oberon
laughed dismissively as one eyebrow winged up. "You of all
people should know. How dare you try to send me into
oblivion. It almost worked, you know. If I had not grabbed
one of the sprites and taken her with me, I would have had
no power to bring myself back. Fortunately for me, and
unfortunately for the sprite, it was just enough magic to land
me deep in the shadow realm instead. Now all of you who
conspired against me shall feel my wrath." His features
tightened and his blue eyes flashed with temper.

Every muscle in Keiran's body tightened, coiled, as if he
were preparing to spring into attack. "You have no business
here in the human realm. Leave now and there will be no
trouble."

Rosalyn's fingers tightened. She had read stories about
Oberon as a mischievous fairy, meddling in the lives of
others. But unlike the stories, Rosalyn could sense something
dangerous building inside this fairy. Magic flared in his eyes
and shimmered around him in a dark red haze as if it were all

too much for his body to contain. The wind kicked up, howling, swirling around those who remained in the rear courtyard. Water dripped from the stone wall surrounding them as spray from the wave condensed.

"The only way I will leave here is with the Fairy Flag. Give it to me or everyone you know and love will die."

Keiran looked behind him to the wall of water that Aria and the others were just managing to keep at bay. "The flag is not mine to give."

"But it is mine." Alastair's voice came from behind them. They turned to see the laird and Graeme had stepped from the relative safety of the castle.

Graeme clutched the Fairy Flag in his hands. "If I wave this flag, the fairy legions will have no choice but to come to the aid of the MacLeods."

Oberon's eyes narrowed thoughtfully. "And pull you back to Fairyland for all eternity."

"That is a debt I am willing to pay if it keeps everyone else safe." Graeme raised his arms, ready to unfurl the flag and send it waving in the wind.

In that moment, Keiran charged, hitting Oberon in the chest with his shoulders and taking him down to the ground. With a howl of rage, Oberon disappeared.

Graeme arrested his movements, halting the use of the flag's last miracle. He released a harsh breath, so great was his relief. "Praise the saints that I did not have to use the flag." As the flag's guardian, once the last bit of magic had been used, Graeme would have been drawn back to Fairyland where he would remain as a prisoner for the rest of his life. It was what the magic of the flag demanded of its flag bearers. And the Duffs had held that position for the MacLeods since the flag had been gifted to them centuries ago.

Alastair helped Keiran to his feet, saying, "I, too, am grateful."

"I was certain—" Rosalyn's voice clouded with tears.

"As was I." Keiran wrapped his arms around her, pulling her close.

In the distance, the wave collapsed, sending a rush of water to crash against the rocky shoreline, but sparing the castle and all those inside its stone walls. Once the roar of the water died down and the loch settled, the waves once again lapped at the shore. The normal sounds of nature returned as though they had never been threatened, with a soft hooting of owls, and the chirping of crickets. And the moon shone down on the castle as it had for centuries.

Aria and the two cloaked figures came to join the rest of them. "Rosalyn, may I introduce you to my sister, Gille, and my mother, Pearl."

Rosalyn smiled at the women who lowered their hoods, exposing their red hair. "Based on how they were able to help you keep that wave away from shore, I assume they also have magic?"

Aria nodded as she went into Graeme's arms. "Mother, Gille, we are so grateful you arrived when you did. How did you know we would need your help?"

"We saw the fire in the village," the younger redhead said. Her face was partially hidden by her hair, but Rosalyn could tell that Gille looked nothing like her beautiful sister. Her features were a bit too angular to be considered alluring, with her slightly pointed chin and cheekbones. But these very angles hinted at an elegance to come, like a rosebud before it bloomed. "We also sensed Oberon's return."

"After we put out the flames, we headed here to warn you about Oberon," Pearl said, her bearing regal. Rosalyn could easily imagine her as the fairy princess from the stories Keiran had told her about the woman who had gifted them with the Fairy Flag.

Silence settled over them as they each reflected on what had transpired. Keiran curled Rosalyn against the warmth of his body. As their heartbeats returned to normal, he broke the silence. "This battle is not over yet."

"I can still feel Oberon's presence on the back of my neck," Aria said, straightening. "Yet we have no idea where he is."

"He must be close, and could pounce on us at any hour," Alastair said, his voice harsh and strained.

Keiran frowned, releasing Rosalyn's waist and shifting his gaze between Alastair and Graeme. "Enough. You are thinking like sheep staked out for a pack of wolves. We have power of our own to use against Oberon."

"Keiran is right." Graeme nodded. "We must stop reacting as Oberon expects us to. Four of us have fairy magic, and the rest of us are a mighty force on our own."

"It is not only Oberon who threatens us," Alastair reminded them.

Aria's gaze lifted to sweep the surrounding area, searching, as always, for a potential threat. "I suspect Oberon predicts we will use our magic against him as we did before, while the English will expect us to come charging into battle, with tempers high and swords drawn."

"Then we should do the opposite," Keiran suggested.

"We are mighty when we choose to be. There is no one better than you at methodical planning, Alastair," Graeme said with a hint of a smile. "Or Tormod, at garnering brute force from our men. Orrick and Aria are skilled warriors, and although Callum is untested, he has shown great promise."

Alastair nodded. "Let us gather first thing in the morning and make our plans when we are rested. 'Tis time for us to turn the tables and become the hunters instead of the prey."

The tension that had come over the men since Oberon's appearance eased. Yet the tension coiling inside Rosalyn increased as Keiran once again shifted his gaze to her. The anger that had momentarily been in his eyes faded, replaced by something darker, more sensual. And honeyed heat flared within her.

Keiran reached for her hand when the others turned and headed back to the keep. His fingers wrapped around hers. His warmth radiated through her body. For a long second, he looked down at her. The moonlight outlined the planes of his face, of his lean muscular body, before he took a step closer, creating a startling intimacy.

He was so close, and yet not close enough. What was it about this man that had captivated her so? Did she feel a connection to him because he had healed her? Or was it because she had seen his true spirit when she had died and left her body? Or was it the way he held her hand? The way his lips moulded so perfectly to her own? Or the gentleness he always showed her when her life had been nothing but neglect and cruelty before he had come along?

"Your hands are warm," he whispered into the night.

Warm? They were melting at his touch. She swallowed roughly as he smoothed his fingers across her palm, her wrist, her forearm, bringing excitement, heat, and hunger.

"Our binding has been removed; though not our obligation to each other. Keiran's gaze was unwavering yet inviting, holding the promise of mysteries yet to be revealed.

Rosalyn's breath faltered as her sense of self-preservation warred with her blossoming desire. A small voice inside her urged her to remain where she stood, that she would end up like her parents if she gave herself over to the passion between them. Another voice reminded her that she and Keiran had joined their lives, no matter how temporarily, and that appeasing passion was her due. If she wanted it.

And heaven help her, she wanted it.

Rosalyn drew a breath and nodded, allowing him to lead her into the castle and up the stairs to his bedchamber.

CHAPTER SIXTEEN

WHEN KEIRAN AND Rosalyn were alone in his chamber, his mouth relaxed into a grin, and he shut the door. The slight widening of her eyes as the latch clicked into place bespoke her nervousness. He allowed himself to visually explore the woman before him. So much of her was still a mystery to him, but now they had time to discover more about each other.

Today he had been surprised by her courage when facing both Lieutenant Long and Oberon. She'd had a newfound confidence that had been lacking in her when they first met. The men in her life would not find her so easy to predict any longer. Perhaps it was the Englishwoman in her that had been her more timid side, and the Scottish woman who was strong and brave had simply been waiting for the right time to emerge.

Two small steps closed the gap between them, bringing her into direct contact with his body. He could not hold back his quick intake of breath that filled the silence of the room. The feeling of her softness against his hardness had him hardening almost to the point of pain. He clenched his jaw, trying to slow down his desire so as not to frighten her as he brought his hands up to her shoulders. His fingers coiled in the silken knot at her crown, removing the pins to allow her hair to fall freely about her shoulders.

He inhaled the scents of heather and moonlight as she lifted her face to his. Staring into her beautiful hazel eyes, he saw not fear but the echo of his own desire. The thought made his heart pound. He slid his hands down her back until he reached the curve of her hips. She held her breath as he bent his face to hers, their bodies touching intimately as he waited motionless for her to bridge the distance between them.

She raised her hands to cup his jaw, then closed her eyes, and pressed her lips to his. His emotions warred inside him as he tasted her sweet innocence, wrapped himself in her touch. It had been far too long since he had last been with a woman. Far too long since he had been unsettled by anything.

And Rosalyn unsettled him in every way. She had captivated him from the moment they had met. He had been assailed by unfamiliar emotions and feelings, half of which he could neither name nor identify. She filled him with more than simple desire or lust. She did something to him he could not comprehend. Part of him wanted to hold her, to kiss her, and the other part wanted to do everything in his power to keep her safe, from Lieutenant Long, from Oberon, from her brother, from even himself. Her physical injuries he could heal, but there were other wounds he sensed in her that ran deep, and he was not certain he could mend them. He broke the kiss and studied her once more. Her gaze reflected trust, making his throat tighten.

"I know you will not hurt me, Keiran, so I willingly give myself to you."

She fitted herself to him, and a shudder racked his body. He took her lips, parting them, and his tongue delved inside. He brought his hands up to pluck at the laces of her dress. When he worked the stubborn laces free, he lifted the gown over her head, then tossed it to the floor.

In return, she unfastened the silver brooch at his shoulder, allowing the tail of his tartan to fall, then deftly unfastened his belt, allowing his sword and tartan to join her dress. He stood before her in only his shirt and boots. While he kicked off his boots and pulled his shirt over his head, tossing it to the floor, she set aside her slippers and hose.

Heady with desire, he pulled her close once more, placing light kisses along her jaw as he slowly lifted the hem of her chemise. The fabric whispered across her abdomen, against her breasts, only to join the rest of their clothing.

She stood naked before him, bathed in only the golden firelight and the warmth of his gaze. His fingers trailed over her abdomen, where the enemy's sword had pierced her flesh. Not a single mark remained. Feeling the need to atone for what had happened to her, he bent and kissed the unmarred skin.

At his touch, she gasped, then closed her eyes. "You made me whole again."

"I healed your wound, Rosalyn, nothing more." He pressed the lightest of kisses from her abdomen to the valley between her breasts. "We are both making ourselves whole again after the misfortune in our lives."

"Making ourselves whole," she whispered into the dimness as she brought her hands to rest on his shoulders.

Warmth pooled in his belly as her caress moved down his back, then to his hips. He nuzzled her breast with his mouth before his lips closed over her taut nipples, first one, then the other. She moaned softly and tipped her head back as he increased the pressure of his languid caress. "If you let me, I will heal you in a different way tonight."

At her questioning gaze, he continued, "Physical touch, even without magic, can give life and express emotion, helping people communicate what they cannot say."

"Is there something you cannot say?"

His fingers trailed down her abdomen. "What does this touch say?"

She pursed her lips, thinking. "Compassion."

He nodded and smiled. "And this touch?" He tapped his fingers over the same sensitive flesh.

"Playfulness?"

"And this?" This time he used long, delicate strokes, then slowly built the pressure as he moved his fingers from her abdomen over her hips and down her thighs.

She inhaled sharply. "Desire?"

He gained his feet and pulled her tight against his body. "Aye, desire. I want you to feel my desire for you, let it sink inside you, let it warm you, and let my touch soothe whatever wounds you still contain."

"And will my touch heal you?" she asked, running her fingers across the rigid muscles of his chest, and lower. Towards the most male part of himself. "Aye, lass. You make me feel things I have never felt before. The old wounds fade away beneath your touch to become something new."

"I am a new creation and if I can take you along on this journey of rebirth, then consider me your willing partner."

He drew in a ragged breath and allowed his hands to span her back, her waist, her hips, and outer thighs. Warmth flared from his hands everywhere he touched. As had happened when he healed her, a spark passed between them, moving from him to her and back again. Did she feel it too? The strange sensation?

Rosalyn opened her eyes, and for a heartbeat he tensed, worried that she would pull away. Instead, she simply looked deeply into his eyes with innocence, tenderness, and passion. The combination fired his blood, racing through him as if a powerful storm had suddenly unburdened itself, swelling a stream into a raging river.

An incoherent sound of anticipation escaped him as he pulled her firmly against him, and another sound followed the first at the sensation of her skin against his own, and the rigidness of his arousal as it nestled into the juncture of her thighs.

In response, Rosalyn slid her fingers over the firm muscles of his chest, his arms, his neck, and shoulders, following each touch with her lips, as he had done. Heat pulsed through him, pulling him into a place without thought, without time, where all he cared about were the waves of sensation and fire cresting through his body, and his desperate need for more. The world around them faded, leaving only the two of them, and the shadows of the night.

"Come with me," he said, his voice heavy with desire. Scooping her into his arms, he carried her to the bed and set her gently in the centre before he settled on his knees beside her. The firelight played across her skin, and copper highlights shimmered in her long brown hair splayed across one of his pillows. He leaned down and breathed deeply in the tumbled mass of her hair, savouring the sweet scent. "You are an enchantress, a goddess, and for tonight, you are all mine."

***

FOR TONIGHT, YOU *are all mine.* The words tumbled through her mind, and a momentary pang of tightness came to her chest. Again, a reminder that theirs was not a permanent connection. She forced the pain aside as he swooped down to capture her lips again. Tonight, she did not want to think of anything except the pleasure he had promised to bring her.

Her fingers slid again over the contours of his well-muscled chest, sprinkled with hair that was so different from her own. She slid her hands down across the ridges of his stomach and down to where his hair surrounded his manhood.

Keiran sat back on his knees, sliding his hands up her calves to the insides of her thighs while her hands sought his long hard shaft that jutted from between his rock-hard thighs. Her hands encircled him. His skin felt like satin and heat radiated from him, spreading through her.

"You are sending me over the edge of madness," he groaned. She could feel his erection pulse and flex instinctively in response to her touch.

She chuckled. "Then join me as I am already there."

He responded with a single savage groan as he eased his hard thighs between her legs, entered her, and filled her body with promise and heat.

She gave a low cry and clutched him with her thighs and hands as his palms held her, sealed her to him. She felt stretched at first, then the tension eased, to be replaced with only a desperate need and a slow-burning fire.

Only when the pain shifted to a flowering sensation did he begin to move, slowly at first, then deeper, filling her more fully with each thrust. And the fire that had smouldered like embers in her belly burst into flames. The heat of it consumed her as she sought whatever it was he tried to give her. Rosalyn felt as though she teetered on the edge of oblivion. The sensations too intense to bear in silence, she cried out as pleasure coiled tighter and tighter inside her with each measured thrust. Instinctively, she arched up again and again, meeting each plunge of his, bringing even more fiery heat.

Heat spiralled inside her, growing stronger and stronger. Instead of experiencing that rapture alone with her eyes closed, she opened them to see raw and unfettered pleasure on the planes of Keiran's face. There was more, as every inch of her body, every fibre of her being filled with warmth and pleasure, she also saw that where they were joined, his maleness to her femininity, their bodies glowed with the same healing light he had used in the forest.

Instead of fear, joy flooded her and with his next thrust all sensation shattered around her, propelling her into the awaiting abyss. A groan escaped Keiran. She held on to him, falling with him over the edge of forever.

He wrapped his arms tightly around her as he shifted to his side, taking her with him, careful not to separate their bodies. The light that they had shared during their bonding faded like the last flickering flames of a candle at the end of the wick.

Her heart thundered in her chest, and she brought her hand up, pressing it over his rapidly beating heart. With him in this moment she felt not only safe and protected, but also cherished and consumed.

Her world had shattered, and yet instead of spent, she

felt renewed. As their heartbeats and their breathing steadied and slowed, Rosalyn rose up on her elbow to gaze down into Keiran's face. In the firelight, she saw an ease in his features, a newfound joy that had not been there before. It was as if something that had been taken from him long ago was somehow now returned. The thought pulled at her heart.

Had the light between them done that? Had his own magic healed him in a way he was not yet aware of? Had it done the same to her?

Her breath caught. When he had healed her before, she had felt not only the healing warmth, but something much deeper that had pulled at her heart, even more than the joining of their bodies, even more than the pleasure still rolling through her. When he had healed her, he had given her a part of himself, and in that moment, when the breath had returned to her body, she had felt his loneliness, his pain, his confusion as to his purpose in this realm, and his fear of not belonging anywhere.

Did a shared touch reveal that much of herself to him? Her breath caught. She had told him only a small portion of her misfortune after her parents died. He had already sensed her loneliness, and she had not hidden her fear of her Scottish half, but did he know about her fears about her father's mental stability? As a young child, she had overhead conversations between her grandmother and her father about his "imbalance of fluids" that caused him to be sad and irritable at times.

When their father and mother were away from the house, their grandmother would arrive with a doctor in tow who would treat them in their beds, bloodletting them to rid the children of their demons. And when that was through, they would plunge her and Hugh into cold baths, and even strategically beat them so the bruises would heal before their parents returned.

Passing his own frustration and abuse on, her brother Hugh had taken his anger out on her. Every day he belittled her, reminding her that she was just like her father, that she would slowly go mad as she aged, and that he would send her to an asylum if she did not cooperate fully with his plans. It was why she had allowed him to send her off to Scotland to marry a total stranger. She had not thought she deserved anything more.

Yet, since coming to Scotland and having to rely on her own wits and the charity of the MacLeods, she was starting to wonder if it was not Hugh who took after their father, and she who took after their mother. Still, she did not want her past to colour Keiran or the rest of his clan's treatment of her. Here, she was free of that part of her life. A part she never wanted to return to. But if the man before her discovered all that, would he break his promise to her to find her a post with another Scottish family?

Because of their handfasting, for the next year, she would stay with the MacLeods and help Gwendolyn and eventually Fiona with their children. But what would happen after that?

Keiran had made it perfectly clear that his offer of protection would expire after the designated length of time.

Snapping her out of her new worries, he reached for her hand, lifted it, and twined his fingers with hers in a tender caress. His gaze met hers, curiosity reflected there. "What are you thinking so hard about?"

Rosalyn's breath eased. He acted no differently towards her. Did that mean he had not sensed her past misfortune? Her self-doubt? Her fears? "About the future." It was the truth. He had asked for that between them.

His smile held a seductive edge as he pulled her to him and rolled her onto her back, releasing her hand. "The future is that I will do my best to distract you from all your thinking." He leaned down and ran his tongue over her nipple.

Heat stung her cheeks as her body immediately responded. She felt herself readying, warming once more at the very thought of him hard and hot within her.

His smile grew. "I see you like the idea. Then let me show you something else that will bring you as much pleasure as before."

He turned onto his back and lifted her on top of him, sliding inside her. His hips moved upwards, and she gasped at the fullness and the pleasure.

His face flushed, his eyes glazing with an expression of primitive desire.

All her thoughts stilled as he thrust deep, quickening the rhythm. This joining was basic, elemental. In only moments, pleasure flared and spilled through her with such intensity that she cried out.

A heartbeat later, he joined her. His raw cry filled the chamber as he spasmed within her, shuddering helplessly as he poured his seed into her body.

She collapsed on top of him. His hips still moved yearningly, as though he did not want to stop though he had reached his satisfaction. A moment later, he lay still, breathing heavily, his hot flesh nestled against her own.

Sweet heavens, the passion between them was more than she ever imagined. And this time, she had been so caught in the vortex of sensations he drew out in her that she forgot to look for his healing light. A quick glance at his face assured her there was no new awareness, and she nestled back against him, allowing her breathing to gradually become steady and slow.

"Rest while you can, my sweet," he said, running his hands along her back. "For I fear I have still not had my fill of you."

She breathed a contented sigh. Tonight, they could pretend the rest of the world did not exist. Tomorrow's realities would rise with the sun and set them on a different, more dangerous path.

CHAPTER SEVENTEEN

KEIRAN AND ROSALYN joined the others in the great hall at daybreak. Alastair and all of Keiran's brothers ate meat pies to break their fast while they studied the map Keiran had retrieved from the Nicolsons in the centre of the table. This time when Keiran looked at the words written on the page, he could easily recognise the place names where the English regiments' locations had been as of several days ago.

Keiran held a chair out for Rosalyn, and as he did, he caught her gaze, hoping she could see the thanks written there for all she had taught him.

At her nod of recognition, he smiled, taking the seat beside her. The men talked between bites of pie about where the soldiers were in relation to Dunvegan.

"Are you all so certain their locations have not changed? We know Lieutenant Long's men are much closer than previously recorded." Keiran reached for a plate and a savoury pie, then passed it to Rosalyn before taking one for himself from the pile.

"I sent four teams of men out an hour ago to verify at least where Lieutenant Long has positioned himself, if not all the regiments. We should know more by the close of day," Alastair said. "Until things are confirmed, we must come up with plans for the English and for Oberon that neither of them would anticipate."

"If we are not going to attack them outright, then how do we draw the English into a trap?" Tormod stood and thumped both hands on the table. "I still say attacking them directly is the better move."

Only Rosalyn flinched at the expression of their brother's frustration. The rest of them had become used to Tormod's irritation at any plan that did not include physical force. Keiran had learned over the past few weeks that swordplay was Tormod's domain in the family. Orrick's strength was in logic. Alastair's strengths were strategy and negotiating peace. Callum tended to sit back and observe. Because of Keiran's magical ageing, the now youngest brother was more comfortable with music and entertainment than with a sword. And as for himself, he was also a strategist. They would have to rely on all those skills to formulate a plan.

"Do we wait for them to come to the castle, or do we meet them away from our walls in some other place we control?" Orrick asked, mulling his own question over with a thoughtful expression. "Rugged terrain will give us the advantage. The English can only seem to fight in linear formations with coordinated musket fire. Yet, those tactics have proven effective against charging Highlanders."

"They have superior firepower, but their uniforms are

heavy, making them less agile," Alastair commented.

"How about we draw them to the shoreline and hide in the boats, then attack when they least expect us to?" Callum offered, leaning forward to engage in the conversation for once.

"Your plan has its merit, Callum," Alastair said calmly. "But it might be hard for us to sneak up on them if we are in the water ourselves."

Callum blew out a breath. "You are correct, as always."

"Keep thinking," Alastair encouraged. "You are on the right track. The shoreline would be difficult terrain for them to hold their lines."

"I have read about the Stone Age hunters digging pits large enough to trap deer and elk. Also, there are Amazonia tribes who capture tapirs in such a manner," Rosalyn's voice chimed in, strongly at first then softening as the men turned to stare at her with curiosity.

Orrick brightened. "I've read such stories as well. It is a practice that has gone by the wayside with the invention of more precise arrows and now muskets."

Alastair's brow knit. "We would need something to draw the English to the area of the trap."

"The trap would have to be set in a valley of sorts, to narrow their lines, forcing them into the pits," Keiran added, warming to the suggestion.

Tormod frowned. "It is a clever idea, except that once the first few men fall into the pit, the rest will avoid it. We will still need to fight them in close combat."

Alastair leaned back in his chair. "We do not need to draw the attention of the entire regiment. The only person we need to capture is Lieutenant Long."

Orrick nodded. "I was concerned about how we would capture a whole regiment and take them up to Dunshee Castle to contain with the rest of our English prisoners. We would have needed the help of our allied clans, and the more people who know our secret, the more likely that knowledge will leak back to England and threaten us all."

"Agreed," said Alastair. "But who or what will we use to draw the English in?"

"Callum could play his mandolin," Keiran said.

"Nay." Callum's eyes widened. "That man will shoot me before I could so much as finish one song." He shook his head. "I want to help, but not at the expense of my life."

Alastair's features brightened. "I never would have believed I would say this, but we could deploy the same trick Garrick MacDonald used against us when he kept Gwendolyn as his prisoner. I still have the large sheet of glass he used to throw her image from one place to another using light. Camera obscura is an old trick that certainly fooled all of us." Alastair turned to Callum. "We could throw your image and keep you safely away from any musket fire."

"That trick was only successful because it was dark in one place and light in another," Graeme reminded them all. "We will have to set the trap at nightfall, and somehow find a way to keep the rest of his regiment from following him."

"I know exactly how we accomplish that task," Alastair said with a smile. "A secret delivery of our finest whisky should do the trick. What man if given the gift of our best whisky would not partake of a sip or two?" His smile increased. "Before that, however, we will have Lottie dose the liquor with her special sleeping herbs. Not only will these men be out of our way, but they won't remember a thing."

Callum pressed his lips together, then smiled. "It would be rather fun to play the man for a fool. And to fill his men's thoughts when they sleep with tall tales so they have no idea what was real or imagined."

"Then you'll do it?" Alastair asked.

Callum nodded.

"What will you do with the lieutenant once you capture him?" Rosalyn asked, her face pale. "I want him to release me from any legal obligation, but it is our Christian duty not to murder him in cold blood as he tried to do to me."

"I have an idea that does not require any bloodshed," Alastair said. "We will need to tempt the lieutenant with something he desires more than winning whatever game he is playing with your life, Rosalyn. Is he the type of man to be tempted?"

"He is shallow and vindictive," Rosalyn said, straightening. "If you dangle a big enough carrot in front of him, he is sure to bite."

"Good," Alastair said with a smile. "I have a friend, William Gordon, the second Earl of Aberdeen, who is a Scottish nobleman and a British statesman. I will send word to him that I wish to purchase a rank advancement for the lieutenant. Do you believe the lieutenant will be tempted by attaining the rank of major with little or no effort on his part?"

Rosalyn gasped. "Such an advancement would cost you a fortune. I could not ask you to spend so lavishly on my behalf."

Alastair's brows creased. "You're family. It is what we do for each other that matters most."

She stood as her face turned ashen. "I do not know how I could ever repay such kindness sufficiently."

Alastair shrugged. "There is nothing to repay. Make Keiran happy and be a part of our clan. That is thanks enough."

She swallowed thickly, nodded, then raced from the chamber with what looked to be tears on her cheeks.

Keiran moved to go after her, but Graeme stopped him with a hand on his arm. "Give her time alone with her thoughts. She has had much to adjust to over the past few days. She needs the womenfolk to help her through this difficulty, not you."

Keiran retook his seat, but his gaze followed Rosalyn until she disappeared through the doorway. "What if the lieutenant refuses your bribe?"

"Then he will be taken to Dunshee Castle," Tormod said, his features hardening. "He will take his rightful place among the rest of our 'English visitors.'"

Orrick held up his hands. "We are losing sight of the bigger issue here." His voice was grim. "Stopping the lieutenant from attacking us might help Rosalyn with her marital issues, but it will do nothing to ease the bigger threat the English pose to us and the other clans."

"You are correct, Orrick," Alastair agreed. "That issue cannot be solved by only the MacLeods. All the clans must be involved in that solution because it could very well lead to a war that might leave a lasting effect on Scotland's people and this country."

"If we are only focusing our attention on the lieutenant and his regiment, then we also must remember that this is a man who agreed to marry a woman then sent soldiers to kill her and her men. How can we trust him even if he agrees to whatever incentive we offer? Will he take the bribe and disappear? Will he take his men with him? Will he promise never to attack the MacLeods? We have no way to enforce his compliance other than take away his offered rank advancement."

"All good questions, Orrick. None of which I have answers to," Alastair replied, his expression matching the seriousness of Orrick's. "We are in a no-win situation at present. All we can do is try to eliminate the immediate threat and live for tomorrow where we have hope of finding a better, more permanent solution to our issues with the English."

Orrick pressed his lips together before saying, "And you are willing to trust that Lieutenant Long will accept this bribe and leave the MacLeods in peace?"

"The man is a snake," Alastair said. "But the one thing he values above all things, as Rosalyn has proven to us, is his own worth."

"Then we agree this is our best plan for now," Tormod summarised.

Alastair nodded followed by Orrick, Graeme, Callum, then Keiran. Once lieutenant Long was no longer a threat, they could shift their attention on defending the entire country.

"Sounds like we have a plan for taking care of the lieutenant," Callum said. "Once we decide on a location, we will be set there. But what about Oberon?"

Graeme turned his gaze to the other men. "Aria and I came to an idea last night based on what we experienced in both the shadow realm and Fairyland when we went to rescue Keiran, and by what Aria knows of the fairies."

Keiran's focus shifted to Graeme, interested to hear his plan. He would find Rosalyn after their discussion and make certain she was well.

"Aria suggested that we throw a costume party here at Dunvegan to celebrate the commitment Rosalyn and Keiran have made to each other. Oberon is certain to find a way to attend in disguise."

Callum frowned. "If he is in disguise, then how will we

know it is Oberon when we try to capture him?"

"Anyone with fairy blood can recognise another," Graeme said. "Aria will be on the hunt for him, but she said in Fairyland when she was a child, he tended to favour costume that made him resemble animals since he often reverts to such a form while out in daylight hours. Is that not so, Keiran?"

"Aye," Keiran replied, realising he would have to be more careful about the animals he rescued from this point forward. Or he might be responsible for giving refuge to the very man they wanted to trap. He did not have the skill of identifying the fae from the human like Aria, her mother, or her sister did. His blood was all human.

Keiran's gaze drifted back to the door through which Rosalyn had departed. His human blood had run hot last night with her in his arms. By the heavens, he wanted to go after her, not only to see that she fared well after her upset, but also to pull her into his arms once more. He could still recall her softness, her scent, the way she trailed her fingers against his skin. He had thought last night would appease his appetite for her, but the more he discovered the nuances of her body and the things that brought her pleasure, the more he craved her. He also realised that he had explored every curve and nuance of her body, but he also wanted to know her thoughts, her dreams, her desires, and he could not do that planning to go to war on two fronts.

It was as if the two sides of himself were battling against

each other, threatening his current situation as a MacLeod, a brother, and husband. If he wanted a life with Rosalyn, then he had to defeat both men who threatened to upset everything. The sooner these men were out of the way and out of their lives, the better.

ROSALYN RACED OUT of the great hall and ran into the front courtyard. Tears stung her eyes and blurred her vision. She drew in a breath of the cool morning air, allowing it to seep inside her, calming the turmoil that Alastair's words had brought forth. He was prepared to spend a small fortune on her to free her permanently from Lieutenant Long. Yet it was the word "family" that had twanged deep inside her. She had not been part of a family for a very long time, and it wasn't until that moment that she realised how much she wanted to be a part of a family again—part of Keiran's family.

She tipped her head back, allowing the wind to caress her face. When the breeze failed to bring the tranquillity she longed for, she focused on the sound of the birds in the trees and the waves that gently lapped at the shore in the distance. Last night, when Keiran had taken her into his arms and held her close, she had felt safe and cared for. But not loved or cherished. The sooner she accepted that, the better off she would be.

Rosalyn forced her breathing into a slow, steady rhythm,

and drew silent strength from the earth beneath her feet. Every day, she seemed to be finding a newfound connection to the land of her mother's people. *Of her people.* The thought brought the sense of calm for which she had been searching. She turned back towards the castle's doorway when she heard a sound that made her pause. She stopped, listening for the noise that seemed out of place amongst the other sounds of the morning.

A soft screech came again, from a distance. Feeling safe within the walls of the castle, she followed the soft sound that seemed to be coming from the gate. As she neared, she saw a splash of black fur and heard a distinctive meow. She knelt before the gate to see a bedraggled kitten. "Sweet baby," she cooed as she reached through the iron bars of the portcullis and lifted the kitten into her arms. The kitten immediately started purring and rubbing itself on her arm. "Are you lost?"

Rosalyn studied the animal's black coat, white paw, and noted a little splash of white on the animal's chin. The feature that drew her attention was the kitten's intense blue eyes.

Could this be another kitten from the mother cat Keiran had found a few nights ago? "You must be starving," she cooed again, rising. With determined steps, she carried the small beast into the castle then back outside and into the rear courtyard where she made her way to the mews.

She opened the door to the small haven Keiran had created for his menagerie of injured animals and moved to find the mother cat nursing her other kitten beneath the table. She held the small, wet kitten out to the mother cat, expecting Midnight to accept the lost kitten. Instead, the animal flinched backwards and hissed, before gathering her nursing kitten closer. Then chaos erupted as the birds in the small space shrieked and flapped their wings, as if they, too, were annoyed with the new visitor. Shivering, the brown rabbit buried itself beneath the hay.

Rosalyn pressed her lips together and frowned. She did not know much about animal behaviour, yet the mother cat and all the other creatures had made their opinion of accepting the new kitten perfectly clear. "Never fear, sweet kitten." She spoke softly to the abandoned animal in her hands. "I will take care of you. Let us go find you some milk, shall we?"

The mother cat was still hissing and growling until Rosalyn shut the door behind her. "Perhaps you need a bath, too." She drew the kitten closer to her nose, not detecting any foul scent. What other reason could the animals have for acting so strangely? She nestled the kitten in the curve of her arm as she continued towards the kitchen. "I will wash you and feed you, and then tomorrow we can try to reintroduce you to the others."

Rosalyn's steps were filled with such purpose, and her focus was on what she would say to Mrs Honey when she arrived at the kitchen, that she did not notice the splash of white on the kitten's chin shifting to the bridge of the animal's nose.

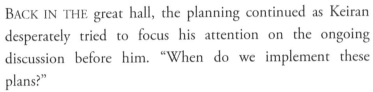

BACK IN THE great hall, the planning continued as Keiran desperately tried to focus his attention on the ongoing discussion before him. "When do we implement these plans?"

"We can start our plans with Oberon this evening. However, we must wait for the scouts to return with the locations of the English regiments before we can execute that plan safely."

"What do we do with Oberon once we have captured him?" Keiran met Alastair's gaze directly.

The heaviness in Alastair's eyes spoke his thought that Oberon would not be easy to capture and even harder to contain. "We have not been able to find a solution to that."

"We could force him into the shadow realm. It would not be a permanent solution, but it could take him days, even years to make his way back here."

"And he will be angry and more dangerous when he finds a way out," Tormod said.

"How would we even get him into the shadow realm?" Alastair asked. "Mother had to help us the last time at great cost to herself. Can we ask her to do that again and possibly lose her for good this time?"

"Haven't we already lost her? Or at least the mother we used to know?" Callum asked with a frown.

"Aye. Mother is much changed from when she was alive, but she has been so helpful in the past few months. Without her early warnings, we might have fallen to more than one foe. Besides, none of us can deny that she is changing. She can touch us now. She can feel emotion. She is less translucent every time we see her." Orrick's brows came together as they did when he was deep in thought. "I suspect it is because she is clawing her way back from the spirit realm where she is trapped and may eventually find her eternal reward in the afterlife. Then, her half-existence in this realm will be at an end."

"Mother?" Tormod called out, hoping to draw the Grey Lady to them. To the table he explained, "I know we all only want what is best for our mother. But before we make assumptions, we should ask her feelings on the matter before we make any further plans."

Answering Tormod's summons, a frothy grey mist swept across the floor of the great hall, then gathered into a more solid shape at the end of the table, until their mother appeared before them. *You called me, my sons?* Her unspoken words filled their minds.

The mist that surrounded her lessened, leaving a more solid version of their mother than had ever been there before. Orrick was right. As the days passed, their mother became more of the woman she had once been. Even so, as she walked behind each of them, placing a hand of greeting upon their shoulders, enveloping them in an otherworldly mist that crawled across their skin, her touch left a chill in its wake. She might appear more human, but she was not fully of this world either.

"Mother," Keiran said. "We need your help. We have a plan to trap Oberon, yet we have no idea how to contain him once he is our prisoner. He cannot die as humans do. Graeme, Aria, and I tried to obliviate him and failed. How do we keep the fairy king contained so that he cannot keep interfering in the lives of the MacLeods now and in future generations?"

Any joy Keiran might have imagined in the Grey Lady's features vanished, replaced by a sombre expression. *There is a way,* she said, her voice almost tortured. *After the last time I helped Aria and Graeme break through to the shadow realm, I almost faded from this realm, until my children pulled me back. Yet as I existed partially in the human realm, and partially in the spirit realm, I realised I can choose my own fate. I can remain here with all of you, or, when I am ready, I can move on to the spirit realm and my eternal reward. I could also shift into the shadow realm, where I would then stay for all eternity. If that is what you need me to do, I can take Oberon with me to the shadow realm.*

"Nay," Callum and Orrick said in unison.

Tormod crossed his arms over his chest. "If you leave us, we want it to be for something better, not for an eternity of pain and suffering at that man's side."

Alastair shook his head, his expression pained. "We can find another way that does not involve you sacrificing yourself, Mother."

I would happily sacrifice what remains of myself to see my children safe.

"Nay," Keiran agreed. "There must be another solution."

In that same moment, Aria raced into the chamber, her face set with a look of determination but also fear. "I apologise for interrupting, but I thought I should tell you this immediately."

"What is it?" Graeme asked, standing, and moving to his wife's side.

Keiran's stomach clenched at the overly bright look in Aria's eyes. Something had not simply frightened Aria, it had terrified her.

"It is only a feeling, but I sensed that Oberon has returned, and not simply to the area. He is in the castle. I cannot sense where or how he accomplished that task, but he is here. The time for planning is over. We must act immediately."

A dark shiver passed through Keiran as he and all gathered at the table stood, ready to spring into action. "I must find Rosalyn and warn her."

Alastair nodded. "The battle has begun. Alert the warriors. I want every nook and cranny of this castle searched for the intruder." He turned to Graeme. "Send me your fastest rider. I need to get that message to the Earl of Aberdeen as quickly as possible to his estate on the Isle of Skye."

Graeme nodded. The men headed towards the door, but stopped when Aria held up her hand, stalling their movements. "There is more," she said, her voice tight.

"Tell us." Alastair's brows creased.

Aria straightened. "One of the scouting parties has returned. Within the hour, Lieutenant Long's men will be at our gates. They have a battering ram and several cannons."

Keiran tensed. "How will we implement our plans now?"

A muscle moved spasmodically in Alastair's throat. "Graeme, Tormod, Callum, the three of you will figure out a way to get the whisky containing a sleeping draught to the Englishmen." To Aria he said, "Find your mother and sister. I need the three of you to be ready with whatever magic you can use to aid us."

When she nodded and raced from the chamber, Alastair turned to Keiran. "Go find Rosalyn, then join Orrick and myself in our search for Oberon." He turned to the Grey Lady. "Mother, we could use your help as well to find the fairy king. You see things we do not."

I will help, she said before vanishing in a swirl of mist.

Their enemy was not only amongst them, but also at their doorstep. "Alastair?" Keiran turned back to his brother from the doorway of the chamber. "There is another way to send Oberon back to Fairyland."

"How?" he asked with a hint of desperation in his voice.

"We use the final magic contained in the Fairy Flag,"

Keiran said, emotions raw. He knew Alastair did not want to be the laird who used the last of the magic it contained. "It would spare Mother and save us all."

"And doom Graeme for all eternity when he is drawn back to Fairyland along with the flag's magic." Alastair shook his head. "I cannot do that to my friend and Aria's husband. There must be another way."

CHAPTER EIGHTEEN

NOT ONCE, SINCE she had died nine years ago in the dungeon of Dunvegan Castle, had Lady Janet Mac-Leod felt like a spirit, until today. With desperate urgency, she flitted through the hallways and corridors, the secret passageways, and parts of the old keep that were still under renovations, trying to locate something, anything that did not belong in the castle. To save time, she vanished through one wall, only to appear on the other side, sometimes startling the residents who were unaware of her frantic activities.

To be thorough, she even checked the dungeon where she had died, finding nothing but horrible memories of a much darker time in her existence. As she moved about the castle, she wondered not for the first time why she had become a ghost at all.

Her husband had been responsible for her death, tossing her into the pit and allowing her to waste away in the darkness until she had begged for death to claim her. As reality had slipped from her at her last breath, instead of seeing a bright white light, she had seen a grey mist forming around her, cocooning her in peaceful serenity, as though softening the harshness of death.

And then, her body had floated up through the slats that covered the pit, stuck in a sort of half-life where she retained her emotions and her memories, yet a lingering sadness settled about her at the thought that her children could still be in harm's way with a father who was no longer rational, and extremely dangerous.

Lady Janet remembered with a hint of amusement how she had taken great pleasure in haunting her husband. Her ability to interact with the physical world had been taken from her, but she had done everything in her power to make certain he did not harm her children.

Since her husband's death, she had started to change. Slowly at first, she had regained small abilities as her children returned to Dunvegan. She could sense their emotions, hear them speak, see them clearly, touch them, and feel their warmth echo against the mist that comprised her form. The thought brought a smile to her lips.

In the last few months, she had been able to not only see all her children again, but also to touch them, hold them, love them as she had longed to do for years. If the opportunity to rid her family of Oberon and his continued vengeance against them presented itself, she would gratefully sacrifice what sliver of her life remained to keep them safe. Nothing mattered more than her children's lives and happiness.

MORNING GAVE WAY to the afternoon as Graeme, Tormod, and Callum added drops of Lottie's sleeping draught to four cases of whisky bottles they had brought up from the cellar. Tormod opened, then resealed another bottle, setting it aside. Later that afternoon, he and Graeme—dressed as peasants—would secretly take a wagon and two horses along the coastline of the loch before turning them back towards the castle. It would appear to the lieutenant's men, setting up camp outside Dunvegan's walls, that he and Graeme were making a delivery for the festivities that night.

"Are you certain you'll be able to outrun the regiment who will set upon you?" Callum asked, uncertainty in his voice.

"Aye," Tormod assured his younger brother. "We'll cut the wagon loose, leaving the whisky behind, and disappear into the woodlands. Once they stop chasing us, we'll head back to Dunvegan the way we left. What can go wrong?"

Callum frowned. "The men could use their cannons before you set that trap. They could surround the wagon, making your regress impossible. They could shoot you from a distance before you have time to retreat. Shall I go on?"

Tormod chuckled, trying to lighten his brother's mood. "'Tis all right, little brother. Graeme and I both know what we must do. We are aware of the risks. And when all this is through, I will show you the best places to hide both in the woods and along the shoreline should you ever need to secrete yourself in the future."

The promise of Tormod sharing his knowledge seemed to lighten Callum's spirit as they filled the final bottle. Tormod stood, then lifted one of the heavy crates. "Let's get these loaded in the wagon. The sooner we implement this plan, the better for us all."

———◦◦◦———

IN THE KITCHEN, Mrs Honey had provided Rosalyn with a saucer of cream, which her newfound friend had eagerly lapped up until his tiny belly had hardened. When the kitten sat back on his hind legs and stared at her with those big blue eyes and a face smeared with cream Rosalyn could not help but laugh. She picked up a nearby towel and cleaned the wee little beast's face. While doing so, she managed to get cream on the bracelet at her wrist. She removed the bracelet and was about to wipe it down when the kitten tottered near the side of the table.

"Hold on there, little one," she scooped the kitten into her arms and held him before her. "You should be more aware of your surroundings." The kitten wiggled in her arms until Rosalyn let him jump down to prowl about the chamber.

"Do ye have plans for the little beast?" Mrs Honey asked.

Rosalyn shrugged. "I had not given it much thought. I

have never had a pet before."

A smile brought out the wrinkles around Mrs Honey's kind eyes. "We'd welcome the little beastie in the castle tae help with the vermin, if ye'd like."

"That's very kind," Rosalyn replied, watching the kitten play with an acorn that had fallen to the floor from a basket nearby that Mrs Honey had been cracking and chopping to add to the stuffing for their supper that evening. The nut rolled across the stone floor, and out the open doorway, with the kitten following right behind. "I had better intervene," she said, chasing after the black and white ball of fur.

Outside, the kitten batted the acorn towards the old keep. Before she could catch up with the animal. Someone must have left the latch not firmly set as the kitten disappeared inside. Rosalyn followed.

A chill came over her as she entered the older section of the castle that Keiran had told her was being restored. She could hardly see a thing in the murky light. "Kitten. Where are you?" Rosalyn searched the darkness and saw a streak of white heading up the stairs.

Instead of chasing the little beast, she paused. Perhaps she should go outside and find a torch or a lantern to light her way. She turned around to do so, when an ungodly yowl came from above. Ignoring her first instinct, she lifted her skirts and raced up the stairs in the hazy grey light.

The sound came again from down the hallway. She entered a chamber that had a soft blue glow inside, yet she could not see any source of light. Another cry came from a doorway in the panelling. Rosalyn reached for her dagger and peered inside.

There inside the hidden passageway was the kitten, sitting quite contentedly in a circle of blue light. The acorn rested at the animal's feet.

She sheathed her weapon before heading inside the passageway. "Come here, you mischievous little trickster. I should name you Hermes for all your cunning and trickery." She bent to pick up the fluffy beast, when it leapt backwards, and instead of a passageway of stone, the scene before her changed and instead of on cobblestone, the kitten ran through a lush green forest.

Rosalyn looked behind her only to find towering trees, their bark gnarled and weathered. Yet it was to their roots that her attention shifted. Colossal and sinuous, they writhed outward from the trunks, forming thick, earthen buttresses that snaked across the ground like slumbering titans. The kitten teetered as it walked along one of the buttress edges.

"What happened? Where am I?" She shuffled backwards, only to trip over the edge of a buttress and fall to the mossy ground. She inhaled slowly, then let the air slide from her lungs. She concentrated on the chill dampness seeping into her body from the bizarre, unexplainable forest floor that had somehow appeared at the hallway's edge. And curled her fingers into the moss. At least the chill and the moss were real, tangible. Nothing else seemed that way at the moment.

Everything had started to change when she had rescued the kitten from the gate. Rosalyn's gaze narrowed on the creature. "Who are you? What are you? Because I begin to understand you are not a cat."

The kitten growled, then vanished in a swirl of grey mist, only to reappear and take the shape of a man.

Rosalyn shuddered. "I should have suspected it was you."

"Hermes?" His deep voice rumbled around her with all the power of thunder from the sky overhead. "You would name me after that paltry Greek god? Why not Loki, the shapeshifter? Or Zeus, the god of the sky and thunder?"

Rosalyn scrambled to her feet, and flexed her hand, ready to reach for her dagger. She swallowed hard and asked, "What do you want?" As the fairy king stepped forward, Rosalyn shifted back, careful to avoid the roots of the trees this time.

"The MacLeods seem to have a soft spot in their hearts for you, especially Keiran." The fairy shrugged. "So you are going to help me take my revenge on him and the others for trying to destroy me."

"I will do no such thing." Rosalyn's mind raced. She had a weapon, but the chances of her using it effectively against the fairy king were minimal. He had magic that he could use to manipulate her a thousand different ways. Her greatest weapon was her mind. She had proven that with all that she had taught herself over the years. Could she use intelligence to meet the fairy king on equal ground? She had to try.

"You say that Keiran and the others tried to destroy you, but it was the opposite from what I heard. Aria, Pearl, and Gille gave you their magic to save you from dying. They were the heroic ones, making that sacrifice for your benefit." Shaking her head, she continued, "You were the one who reneged on their sacrifice by draining the very life forces out of their bodies."

His lips pressed into a thin, hard line. "It was my due."

"Was it?" Rosalyn asked. "Or was it you who pushed all the fairy folk to do what came next . . . when they all rebelled against you?"

His gaze narrowed, and with a flick of his hands the forest vanished and instead, an instantly distressed Rosalyn found herself on a towering rock, in the middle of a foaming sea. The shale beneath her feet was wet, and she had to widen her stance to keep from slipping off the rock and plunging into the sea. The fairy king hovered above the rock, watching her through his slitted gaze.

With a thunderous roar, a wave crashed against the defiant monolith. Water exploded against the rock face, sending an icy plume skyward. As it did, the spray caught the light, briefly creating a dazzling rainbow before it was whipped away by the wind, leaving white foam to ripple around the rock in a frenzy of bubbles.

Rosalyn shivered at the spray that drenched her clothing and the salty spray that stung her face. "It is a brave man who can admit he was wrong."

"I am never wrong," Oberon said, glaring at her as another wave crashed against the rock. "And when you die in your dreams, you die in life."

"If this is a dream, can I not just wake up?"

"There is no one to wake you." He smirked. "They are all fighting their own battles. When I take revenge, I am thorough."

She was not the only one caught in Oberon's trap? The weight of her situation and those of the MacLeods felt like a crushing weight on her shoulders. She looked around her for an escape that simply wasn't there. The air vibrated with the raw power of nature as another wave crashed over the rock. The shale beneath her feet was slick and smooth, giving her nothing to wedge herself into or grasp for support. She could feel her feet being inched backwards towards the edge of the rock. It would not be long before she tumbled into the sea.

Keiran was not coming to save her. No one was coming to save her. If she was to survive, she would have to save herself.

As THE MINUTES ticked past, Lady Janet continued her frantic search for Rosalyn. When she approached the old keep for the second time, it was to see that where the grand structure once stood, colossal vines grew like emerald ropes wrapped around the stone building, keeping all who approached out, and trapping anyone inside.

Fortunately for her, such barriers were easy to breach. With ease, she sailed through the roots and stone. Oberon had to be inside, as did Rosalyn. The fairy king would not have gone to such extremes if she were not.

Floating up the stairs, Lady Janet saw a strange blue light emanating from a room down the long hallway. She hurried inside, searching, then paused at the open door to the secret passageway.

Rosalyn!

A chilly dampness leached onto her mist, feeding the dark cold that hovered around her. If she'd had a true body, she would have shivered as she moved towards the blue light, fearing the worst, preparing for anything.

When she saw Rosalyn standing there on the cobble-stones, something inside her soared. Rosalyn was unharmed, standing as though she were waiting for something. Yet as Lady Janet moved closer, her elation turned to fear. Rosalyn stood frozen in place, her eyes open, but her focus was on something that was not of this realm. The young woman neither blinked nor breathed. *Was she dead?*

Lady Janet instinctively wrapped her arms around Rosalyn. The cold surrounding Lady Janet deepened. *Poor dear. What has Oberon done to you?* From within her mist, Lady Janet could sense an awareness, a presence still inside the frozen body that she held so tightly, hoping to convey some comfort, some warmth. After a long moment, she pulled back as a strange sensation further twined with her mist. The sensation blossomed and grew, until she could recognise the emotion that did not come from herself, but from Rosalyn. *Sorrow.* The young woman had communicated her sorrow.

Lady Janet gasped and released Rosalyn only to bring her hands up to cover where her heart had once beat. She had always been able to sense the emotions of others, but never feel them herself. Sorrow reverberated within her mist. *Emotion.* At the intensity of it, she closed her eyes and felt moisture gather behind her eyelids. A tear slipped down to fall on her translucent cheek. *I must find Keiran. Rosalyn is in terrible danger.*

CHAPTER NINETEEN

A KNOT OF fear tightened Gwendolyn's throat as she looked at the Fairy Flag behind the protective glass in the castle's drawing room. At the speed of a spider weaving its web, the thread woven to create the magical artifact slowly unravelled, leaving a fringe of yellow silk at the bottom of the flag and strands of thread at the bottom of the frame. What they once thought was protected was suddenly coming apart.

"That cannot be good," Fiona said, frowning at the treasured flag. "What shall we do?"

"I sent for our fairy sisters," Gwendolyn said. "Perhaps they can do something before the flag disappears before our eyes."

At the mention of their names, the three women she had sent for entered the chamber. "What is it, Gwendolyn?" Aria asked as she, Pearl, and Gille rushed into the chamber. "The maid said you asked to—" Aria's eyes went wide. "What is happening to the flag?"

"I do not know. That is why I called you." Gwendolyn turned to Pearl. "Is this magic?"

She nodded. "Oberon's, I fear."

"Can you stop it?"

Pearl frowned and brought her hand up to the glass. "This is old magic. I fear I cannot stop it—only Oberon can do that. Though I can slow it down."

"You must," Aria said, anguish in her voice. "Graeme's survival is linked to that flag. If it disappears from this realm, so will he."

"Anything you can do," Gwendolyn begged. "The honour and the very existence of the MacLeod clan rests in the fibres of that flag."

Pearl closed her eyes, and let her magic flow from her hands, through the glass, and into the flag she had at one time given to the MacLeods. "My daughters, sing with me the MacLeod fairy lullaby to lull this magic to sleep."

Aria and Gille stood beside their mother and in melodic voices sang the song that the fairies sang to the infant Iain Cair when Pearl had been forced to leave him in the human realm centuries ago. Slow and calming, the song wove through the chamber, expressing tenderness and protectiveness in the depth of melody. To Gwendolyn's gratification, the song stopped the unravelling down to an imperceptible rate.

Gwendolyn's tension eased. The Fairy Flag was safe for now even as so many other dangers loomed on the horizon.

As soon as the song stopped the flag from unravelling, Gwendolyn noted that Fiona's features were pinched, and she kept fidgeting with her arm. Concerned something might be wrong with her or the child she carried, Gwendolyn moved to Fiona's side. "Is anything wrong?"

Fiona drew a ragged breath. "My arm itches. It is almost unbearable." She pulled the sleeve of her gown back to show the red welts that now dominated her wrist and forearm around her silver bracelet.

"Oh, my goodness," Gwendolyn breathed as she reached for the bracelet, removing it from Fiona's arm. "You are clearly having some sort of reaction to the metal." Gwendolyn set the bracelet aside and with an arm about Fiona's waist, ushered her from the chamber. "We must find Lottie and see if she has a tisane or an unguent to help with that swelling."

MOMENTS LATER, THE clatter of hoofbeats sounded along the shoreline. Alastair moved to the sea gate, pleased to see a man in the MacLeod tartan riding towards the castle. It had to be the lad he'd sent earlier in the day to find William Gordon, the second Earl of Aberdeen. Alastair opened the sea gate, then followed the man up into the rear courtyard. The rider reined to a halt and handed Alastair a folded and sealed missive. "I rode as swiftly as I possibly could without endangering the horse."

"Thank you, good sir," Alastair replied, breaking the seal,

then smiling. His friend had agreed to help the MacLeods in gaining a new commission for the lieutenant.

Finally, the tide was turning in their favour.

No sooner had the thought formed when a sharp crack and a slow whistling sound came from the front courtyard. Alastair tucked the missive into the top folds of his kilt, drew his sword and raced for the front courtyard just as a deafening boom, like a massive thunderclap, sounded.

He reached the front courtyard just as a giant crash sounded against the north curtain wall near the old keep, shattering the stone wall. Debris flew in all directions, causing the men in the courtyard to take cover from the projectiles. The sound of the explosion reverberated through the castle, bringing men rushing from inside, weapons at the ready. They raced through the dust and smoke to greet the roaring English soldiers pouring through the smouldering breach.

Keiran appeared beside Alastair. "Was that rider who I hoped it was?"

"Aye," Alastair replied as they ran together towards the onslaught of men.

"Then you focus on wending your way through these men to reach the lieutenant," Keiran said over the thunder of footsteps entering the castle grounds. Formations of red-coated soldiers approached like a red wave seeking the shore, rifles firing.

Some of the castle's warriors fell to the ground, while

others ran for cover. "The sooner you negotiate with the lieutenant, the better off we will all be," Keiran shouted, surging ahead, providing cover for Alastair to reach what remained of the castle wall.

BEFORE THE ENGLISHMEN could advance any farther, a cry from the tower above erupted out of the chaos. The *cath-ghairm*, the blood-curdling call of the Highlanders was followed by "Attack!"

As he ran, Keiran looked up to see Aria and her archers. They rained down volley after volley of arrows, until the enemy was so rattled as they searched for cover that they momentarily stopping their gunfire, giving the MacLeod warriors a chance to move in closer, where English firepower would no longer be effective. The English would be forced to use either bayonets or swords, putting the two sides on more equal ground.

Behind Keiran the skirl of a bagpipe filled the air, the sound fierce and threatening. As were the hundred men dressed in the MacLeod colours. Their faces wore looks of determination. Keiran smiled. In that moment, he and his people looked like the barbarians Rosalyn had been told to fear. He pushed thoughts of her aside as he and the warriors swept across the rubble-strewn courtyard, surging with all their power towards Lieutenant Long's regiment.

Everywhere, battle ensued. Arrows continued to reach targets in the distance, while bladed warriors engaged those already in the breach. All around them came the clangour of steel against steel and the cries of men and horses.

Keiran fought his way through the melee until he came to a large English soldier who sneered at Keiran as he approached. Usually before a battle in Fairyland, Keiran had always felt alone. It was him against death—a human in a magical realm, surrounded by magical creatures who were long-lived and hard to kill. And even though he had been given the gift of healing, a mortal wound would have taken him, as he doubted any fairy would care enough to heal him.

In the human realm, he was the one with the advantage, although if he was badly wounded, he would die like all other men. And he was at peace with that. There were things in this world worth fighting for and dying for. His thoughts turned to Rosalyn, and suddenly with utter clarity, he knew the path his life must take after this battle was through. He needed peace, security, and most of all love.

The last word brought a hitch to his breath. Did he love Rosalyn? Before he could savour the emotions he felt in answer to that question, the Englishman advanced. As soon as this conflict was through, he would find Rosalyn and tell her his true feelings. But for now, he had a job to do. Keiran quickly forced all thoughts of his bride into the back of his mind. "Leave this land in peace," Keiran said as the man dropped into position. "Go back to England and never darken Scottish lands again."

As they circled each other, taking measure of the other, the Englishman laughed. "It is our destiny to conquer the Scots. I'll not walk away from this fight to cleanse the land of all of you." The man lunged.

Keiran parried and spun to the right. The Englishman brought his sword around in a sideways sweep, but Keiran was ready. His blade arched up and back, stopping the man's slice. As the swords collided, Keiran kicked, catching his opponent in the stomach, sending him staggering backwards.

The Englishman regained his feet. He grinned at Keiran. "A worthy opponent at last."

As the two men sized each other up once more, another sharp crack sounded, followed by a slow whistling. Men around them scrambled left and right as a cannonball hit the castle to the right of the drawbridge with a terrific bang and then an explosion.

Keiran relegated the larger chaos to wait for a bigger slice of his attention until after the present acute skirmish with the Englishman was through. He kept his body low as he watched the Englishman's body for his next move. He did not have to wait long. The man's blade arched towards Keiran in a disembowelling sweep, the blood grooves on the blade whistling their deadly melody. To no avail, as Keiran had dropped back and let the blade swing through the empty space where his body had just been.

The Englishman was mighty, but Keiran was quick. And

most of all, his opponent was arrogant, and too confident. Superior weaponry was not all in battle. Speed, wit, and skill could never be taken away. Arrogance, however, could be exploited.

Testing his theory, Keiran stumbled, and watched the man's eyes gleam at his own superiority. Yet with that arrogance came Keiran's opportunity. His opponent swung his sword wide. Keiran jumped inside the opening and drove his elbow into the Englishman's face. With a half turn, the razor edge of his sword slid past the Englishman's arm and into his side.

The invader's eyes flared in pain, but still his sword slashed in retaliation, clipping Keiran's thigh, then coming up to slash at his arm. Keiran blocked the strike with the silver bracelet at his wrist. The metal had protected him from injury, but the band had been cleaved in half.

He fell to the ground on both knees. His silver bracelet landed in two pieces beside him. Despite the Englishman's own bleeding wound, he brought his sword up, clearly preparing to sever his Scottish foe's head from his neck.

Keiran concentrated all his strength into his good leg, and tried to force himself to stand, but before he could a familiar grey mist preceded the appearance of the Grey Lady at his side. The Englishman, so brave in the heat of battle, shrieked and ran away.

Keiran stood, ignoring the pain in his thigh, turning to his mother with a welcoming smile. "Never did I think I would use you as a weapon during battle. My thanks."

Instead of smiling in return, her face remained taut, worried. *Keiran, you must come with me. It is urgent.*

"You found Rosalyn?"

I did, and what I found is not good. Come. We must hurry.

Keiran followed, limping as fast as he could. Then he stopped. He could go much faster if he took a moment to heal his wound. Lady Janet continued on. Gathering his energy, he placed his hand on his wounded thigh and allowed the light from his hands to soak into his leg, knitting muscle, mending flesh until all that remained of his injury was torn fabric and a scar that would continue to fade with time.

Making up for lost time, he raced as fast as he could towards the old keep where his mother stood waiting. Keiran skidded to a stop and gaped at the entirely new and vast vines covering the walls of the castle. Another crack sounded, followed by a low whistling. Keiran turned to see a cannonball headed straight for the old keep.

"Mother! Take heed!" He reached for her on instinct, only to have his hand pass through her. He made to seek cover, when one of the vines detached itself from the keep and rose up like a giant arm, smacking the cannonball back at the English to defend itself from harm. It exploded with a deafening crack, taking out the very cannon that had sent it towards Dunvegan.

"Are you controlling the vines, Mother?" Keiran asked,

baffled at what had just happened.

Nay, my son. I believe the vines are defending themselves. As if to prove her point, the giant vine shifted over the Englishmen and came down with a splintering smack on the second cannon, toppling the weapon, and sending several Englishmen flying, while others scattered into the woods. The Grey Lady, deliberately using her ghostliness to scare the enemy, flitted after them, looking more fearful than she usually did around her family, making certain the men did not return anytime soon.

When she floated back to Keiran, it was with a smile. *I have never actually frightened anyone but your father until today. I rather enjoyed it. And, best of all, the Englishmen paused in their flight to take the cases of whisky you boys set in the woods for them to find.*

"That is good." Keiran turned back to the vine-covered doorway. He drew his sword and raised his blade to strike.

Stop! his mother warned, her smile vanishing. *Based on what happened with the cannon fire, we know these vines are enchanted and will protect themselves when provoked.*

Keiran sheathed his sword. "Then how will I reach Rosalyn? She is inside, is she not?"

Aye. She is there. I can pass through the stone, though you cannot. Lady Janet pursed her lips. *Plants like sunlight, water, and rich soil. Perhaps we can tempt the vines away from the doorway with water, long enough for you to get inside the keep.*

Keiran nodded. "I shall return." He raced for the well in the rear courtyard and drew a bucket of water before returning to the front courtyard. He dipped his hand in the pail and brought his fingers to dangle over the thick vine, sprinkling water on the surface. When the vine shifted, Keiran repeated the drops, until the vine let loose its hold, searching for more water.

He set the pail at a distance, then watched as the vine released its hold on the doorway even more, as though sensing a larger quantity of water. While the vine was distracted, Keiran slipped through the entrance. Lady Janet followed behind.

Keiran's throat was tight as he raced up the stairs. He took each step more swiftly than the last, until he came into the chamber with an odd blue light. From below, the cries of men and the billowing of bagpipes cut through the silence of the old keep, telling Keiran the tides of battle had turned in their favour. Yet it was not joy that gripped him as he raced into the secret passageway his mother indicated before, but despair as he came to a halt in front of Rosalyn. She was as still as a statue, and as grey as death.

He reached out to gently stroke her cheek. Her skin was as cold as ice. "How am I supposed to help her, Mother?"

I do not know. I had hoped you would know how to save her.

Keiran felt his despair give way to anger. He balled his hands, letting his anger build, when suddenly a voice inside him whispered the words he and Rosalyn had read from the Book of Corinthians the other day: *Love bears all things, believes all things, hopes all things, endures all things.* And heals all things, Keiran added.

He relaxed his hands and turned up his palms. From the moment they met, he and Rosalyn had shared a spark, a special connection, which defied understanding. His magic should not have had such a strong response from a human, but it had.

He studied the curve of her cheeks and the set of her chin, defiant even in the face of danger. She was so fragile, and yet also strong. The thought brought a splash of warmth back into his soul. He could use the connection they shared to try to help her, heal her.

He closed his eyes and gathered all his strength, then opening his eyes, he wrapped his arms around her and held her tight as he splayed his hands across her back. Warmth flowed from his hands into her body. He would give her everything inside himself—his strength, his determination, his healing warmth, and his love.

The word came back to him. *Love.*

Joy cascaded through Keiran, intensifying the warmth that flowed from his hands. He had no idea what darkness Oberon threatened her with or where he had taken the cognisant part of the woman in his arms. But he would stay with her, helping her defy whatever torment Oberon had concocted. She was the one who would have to fight, but she would know—even through the veil that separated them— that she was not alone.

CHAPTER TWENTY

A S THE HAZY light of dusk fell over the land, Alastair picked his way through the rubble strewn across the courtyard. The castle was no longer secure. He had placed several warriors to guard the breach, but most of the men were busy tending the wounded or burying the dead. So much destruction and pain caused by one man who wanted someone he could no longer have.

Lieutenant Long would no doubt make a second attack on the castle once his men regained their nerves. Fisting his hands, Alastair stepped through the ragged hole in the curtain wall. He tried to think of something besides the death and destruction wrought this day. There was no time for despair. He needed to stay focused and in control while he moved out to and negotiated with Lieutenant Long for the sake of his clan.

Alastair knew he took a risk, heading for the enemy alone, but he had put his men in enough danger this day. The thought had barely formed when Tormod and Graeme appeared on either side of him.

"You did not think we would let you face that man

alone, did you?" Graeme asked, falling into step beside the laird.

"I had hoped you would stay behind and help the others," Alastair said, then added, "But I do thank you for always standing beside me."

"Let us go get this over with," Tormod said, clutching the pommel of his sword as they approached the eerily silent English campsite that had been set before their conflict had begun.

Watchfires had been set, but not yet lit around the sprawling camp. The activity Alastair had expected after a battle retreat was non-existent. Instead of caring for their wounded or burying the dead, the men lay on the ground, asleep.

To test that theory and to make certain it was not a trap, Alastair lifted a man's arm and let it fall. No response. Still not fully convinced, he found a stick and poked another man in his most private area and garnered no response. Alastair allowed himself a smile of satisfaction. It would have been difficult to fake unconsciousness with a thrust to that area if the man were not fully dosed with the augmented whisky and sleeping.

Feeling more secure about their safety, they moved about the camp. "Perhaps we can simply find the lieutenant and transport him back to England," Graeme suggested.

"He would only return." Alastair continued to search the faces of the men they passed. There were too many of them to take to Dunshee castle. They would have to determine another way to dissuade them from returning to Dunvegan.

Alastair, Graeme and Tormod walked through the camp for several more minutes until they came to a campfire that had been lit. A single man stood before it, staring into the flames.

As they approached, Lieutenant Long turned to them, and raised his pistol. "I can only shoot one of you before you reach me. But at least I will have the satisfaction of knowing one of you will join me in hell."

"No one has to die this day," Alastair said, stepping forward, making himself a more accessible target than his brothers.

Lieutenant Long kept his pistol aimed at Alastair's chest. "Another ploy? You have already drugged my men. You sent fantastical vines to toss our cannons. What else do you have in store for me?"

Alastair slowly moved his hand inside the tail of his tartan and withdrew the missive the rider had brought back from the Earl of Aberdeen. "I have an offer for you. One you will find hard to refuse." He held out the folded parchment as he stepped ever closer.

A deep frown cut across the lieutenant's face. "What kind of trick is this now? I open the parchment and it explodes in my face?"

Alastair unfolded the paper. "No tricks. I come to offer you a promotion to the rank of major in the British Army."

The pistol wobbled in the lieutenant's hands. "Why would you do such a thing? There must be some concession you would like me to make."

"There is," Alastair replied, moving to stand before the man. "You put away your pistol, then promise to leave Scotland, break your betrothal to Rosalyn, and never attempt to see or speak to her again, and the commission is yours."

The lieutenant's gaze shifted to the parchment in Alastair's hand. "How did you accomplish this?"

"I have friends in high positions in the English government."

The lieutenant pressed his lips together as he released the cock of the pistol then shoved it into his belt. He snatched the parchment from Alastair's hand. His eyes flared as he read the words written there. "There are no strings attached?"

"None that I have not already mentioned. But with those three things, you must comply."

The lieutenant looked beyond Alastair to Graeme and Tormod. "What if the British Army sends me back to Scotland?"

"As a major, you would have some say in your placement," Alastair replied. "See that it is not Scotland. Besides, there are other conflicts around the world where your skills might be better suited."

"My skills." The lieutenant laughed. "If I accept, how do I know you will not attack me as soon as I turn my back on the three of you?"

"You have our word as Scots. We say what we mean." Alastair's voice was hard. "Your future, for Rosalyn's life. What will it be?"

The lieutenant palmed the parchment and turned, running for the trees where a lone horse waited. Alastair and his brothers waited until the sound of hoofbeats faded into the distance.

"Will he stay away, do you think?" Graeme asked.

"I believe he will, though others will come in his stead. Our conflict with the English is far from over."

Tormod looked around the campsite at all the sleeping men. "What will we do with these soldiers?"

"When they discover their leader has abandoned them, they will most likely return to England," Alastair said.

"And tell the tale of an enchanted castle, no doubt," Graeme said with a sigh.

"That is where we come into play," Orrick's voice came from behind them.

The three men turned to see Orrick and Callum approaching the campsite. "We have come to make certain they all believe what happened today was simply a bad dream."

Callum carried his mandolin, but as they had discussed earlier, they did not carry the plate of glass with them to throw Callum's image. At Alastair's questioning gaze, Callum replied, "We tested the image-throwing outside before coming out to join you, and the trick did not work with so much light we did not control. It will be up to the four of you to protect me as I wander through the camp, lacing these men's dreams with suggestions of fairy stories that will make it hard for them to recall what was real and what was not. Even if they do remember some of what happened here, no one back home would ever believe such muddled and fantastical tales."

"I hope you are correct," Tormod said with a frown.

Callum's brows knit as he moved his mandolin into position to play. "You know a lot about war, Tormod." Callum strummed the strings, filling the air with a bright, twangy, and high-pitched melody. "However, I know a lot about music and dreaming."

Without waiting for a response, Callum strolled about the campsite. His music held a sweet and lyrical quality. As Callum walked, he sang of fantastical beasts and the fairy stories their mother had always told them of at bedtime when they were children.

Listening to Callum sing the songs of their youth, Alastair realised that the legends surrounding the MacLeods and the fairy realm reflected that interconnectedness of the two entities. The world of the fae survived and flourished because of the MacLeods' belief. And the MacLeods thrived and were made strong by the protection of the fae and by intertwining with them.

Perhaps that is what they needed to communicate to Oberon to make the fairy king see that together, humans and fairies were better together than they were apart. He turned to Tormod and Graeme. "Stay and protect our brother. I must go see Keiran. I have an idea that might help us in our battle against Oberon."

IN THE FADING light of the day, Aria stared at the vines that had wrapped themselves around the old keep. "This must be the work of Oberon."

"Only he would think to bar those who live here from accessing their own home," Gille agreed.

"It is the fairy king's trap all right," Pearl said, sniffing the thick vine in front of her. "I can smell the magic on the fibres within the plant."

Gille frowned as she tried to wrap her hands around one of the overly large vines. It was bigger than her two hands put together. "How will we move this plant? You saw what happened when the English accidentally struck one part of it with rubble. It retaliated."

"Keiran was able to tease one vine away from the door-way with water," Aria said. "Perhaps we could do the same? Mother, you and I can bring water to the plant like a carrot on a string. Hopefully it will follow when we lead it away from the keep and into the garden outside of the gates."

"I have a better idea, one that might help the vines find a permanent home here at Dunvegan." Pearl moved over to where the vine had sprouted and lifted a handful of dirt into her hands. She ran the gritty soil through her fingers, feeling the composition of the dirt. "The soil here is poor." She turned to her daughters. "I suggest we get a wagon of dirt from the garden or the forest floor that is dense with nutrients and lure the vines away with that."

"I can secure a wagon and horses," Aria said, gazing at the purple and grey light that warned of looming darkness. "Whatever we do, we must do it quicky."

"I will go to the edge of the forest and identify the richest soil," Gille said.

"Mother, would you ask the men to bring several torches?" Aria asked. "I will gather the wagon and horses and meet you both at the edge of the trees." Moving the vines would only be the first and possibly easiest part of unravelling the trap Oberon had no doubt set for Rosalyn, Keiran, and anyone else worthy of his wrath, Aria thought as she headed for the stables.

It did not take long to hitch the horses to the wagon. Aria guided the equipage through the gates and to the area of the woods now illuminated with torches. Several of the warriors stopped their work collecting rubble to help the women fill the wagon with soil quickly. Then, instead of heading back to the castle, the same warriors carried the torches into the garden where Gille had prepared a spot between the round garden and the water garden that Fiona had been working on over the past several months. The two distinct gardens were starting to take shape under her direction.

Half of the soil was spread on the ground where they wanted the vine to situate itself. The other half of the soil was shovelled out as the wagon rolled back towards the keep, leaving a trail of dirt behind. Only a few handfuls of dirt remained when they came to a stop beside the vines. After asking one of the warriors to take over for her as the driver, Aria jumped down from the bed of the wagon with her two hands filled with dirt and sprinkled it on the largest branch she could reach.

In the pale torchlight, the branch quivered, as though responding to the stimulus. A tendril reached out, searching for more. It coiled and stretched until it reached the dirt on the ground, then slowly the entire branch released its grip on the keep, slithering along the path they had laid.

One after another, the branches released the keep, until the entire plant crept along the path like an oversized spider in the moonlight towards the space Aria had planned. When the base of the plant settled into the layer of rich soil, it perforated the ground with roots, anchoring itself in place. And, with a final quiver, it unfurled its leaves and ceased its movements, acting as though it were like any other plant in the garden.

While Aria, her mother, and sister stood, basking in their success, the warriors who had helped them returned to the castle. Aria closed her eyes and allowed the silence of the night to flow around her. For centuries now, she had been trying to understand Oberon. She had studied him, trying to learn his vulnerabilities. And every time she thought she had him figured out, he surprised her. Would this be the last test the fairy king would throw their way?

Even as the question formed, she dismissed it. Rosalyn and Keiran were both missing. The fairy king was no doubt responsible for that, meaning their battle with Oberon was far from over.

At the sound of footsteps behind her, Aria opened her eyes and turned to see one of the warriors running towards them. The torch in his hands illuminated his overly bright eyes. "What has happened?" Aria asked.

"Now Fiona is missing," the warrior said, his voice raw.

A dark shiver passed through Aria. *Oberon!*

CHAPTER TWENTY-ONE

ROSALYN CURLED HER toes against the shale beneath her feet, trying for a few moments longer to keep herself from sliding into the foaming sea. She had tried making Oberon see the error of his ways, but without success. Perhaps it was time for her to appeal to his vanity instead. "If you kill everyone who you feel has ever wronged you, then who will be left for you to rule over? If they are all gone, you will be the king of no one. The king of nothing. And you will cease to be of any importance in either the human or fairy realms."

Oberon's eyes widened as he stared at her with a mixture of surprise and irritation. "I will find new subjects."

"Where?" Rosalyn latched on to the weak logic she had exposed. "All of Fairyland will turn against you when you take your revenge on their mothers or fathers or children."

"I will steal human children and make them my new sons and daughters. I will start with the MacLeods." Oberon's blue eyes glittered dangerously but behind the danger there also lingered doubt.

"Humans do not give up their children so easily. If you

take another of the MacLeod children, it will be you who suffers in the end. With Aria and other magical helpers, the MacLeods will be especially diligent in protecting future offspring," she said with a renewed confidence.

"You think you understand humans and fairies so well, do you?" A ruddy flush came to his cheeks. "On one hand, you would have me forgive those who wronged me, or have me admit I was wrong. On the other hand, you claim humans, especially the MacLeods, will fight with their last breath before losing a child to me again."

"Now that they know it was you who took Keiran from them nine years ago, yes. They will fight you and win."

Oberon's gaze narrowed. "Are you willing to stake your life on that?"

It was Rosalyn's turn to frown. "What are you saying?"

"I propose a game. You against me."

What did she have to lose? If she remained here in this unreal but yet treacherous seascape much longer, she would die. "Explain this game."

"I hide something for you to find. I will give you a map with clues as to its location." He snapped his fingers and an hourglass appeared. "If you can find the object before the sand runs out, I will no longer seek revenge on the MacLeods and the fairies who tried to kill me."

"And if I fail in this quest?" she asked.

He smiled a calculating smile. "I get to keep Fiona's baby and any children you and Keiran might produce."

A shiver raced down Rosalyn's spine. "No, keep Fiona and her child out of this."

He snapped his fingers again. "Too late."

Fiona appeared beside the fairy king, floating above the slippery rock that was still relentlessly pounded by the sea. Terror filled Fiona's expression as she looked about her, biting back a scream.

"Return her to Dunvegan," Rosalyn challenged.

"She is already a player in this game, so, no." The fairy king shrugged. "I will allow you a helper." He snapped his fingers a third time and Keiran appeared, hanging suspended above the churning water near Fiona.

"No!" Rosalyn's heart soared at seeing Keiran once more, even as desperation constricted her throat. "Not Keiran. Have you not tortured him enough for one lifetime?"

Oberon laughed. "Would you like me to bring someone else into this game?"

"No," she said, forcing a calmness she did not feel. How had Keiran survived such deviousness for so long? "If we are to play a game, then let it not be here. Take us somewhere we will not have to fight the environment as well as you."

"Done." Oberon snapped his fingers and instantly she stood in the centre of the fairy circle where she had come face to face with Oberon for the first time. "You seemed to like this place."

Rosalyn looked around her. Keiran was still suspended above the ground by Oberon's magic, and Fiona . . .

Rosalyn's heart thundered in her chest. "Where is Fiona?"

Oberon's gaze became steely. "She is the object you and Keiran will have to find. If you do not, her baby is mine." The fairy king snapped his fingers once more. A map appeared at her feet. Keiran tumbled to the ground. Oberon vanished.

She had no choice but to play this cruel game with the fairy king. Fiona and her babies' lives depended on it.

Keiran rolled to his feet. His gaze shifted to her. His brown eyes warmed, and the hint of a smile pulled up the corner of his lips. A moment later any pleasure she imagined there vanished, and a sombre expression took its place. "Are you really here?" Concern laced his voice as he closed the distance between them and pulled her into his arms. "Oberon did not hurt you?"

Fear and longing shimmered through her. Only moments ago, she had thought she would never see him again. "I am well, though I am not certain for how long. Oberon is using us as bait in a cat-and-mouse game." She pulled out of his arms to pick up the map at her feet. "He has hidden Fiona. We must find her."

Keiran looked at the map in her hands and smiled. "You know why he brought me to you?"

She shook her head.

"He thinks I cannot read. That you will be alone in trying to find Fiona and that you will fail."

At the confidence in his gaze, a hope blossomed inside

her. "And he has no knowledge of the fact that the women of the castle have been teaching me about fighting and strategy." She moved her hand over her skirt and patted where her dagger was sheathed, only to feel nothing. "My dagger."

Keiran brought his hand down to his scabbard, looking up sharply. "My sword is missing as well." He frowned. "When I found you back at Dunvegan you were as still as a statue, and yet when Oberon brought me to you, you were perched on a rock in the middle of a churning sea. On the earthen plane, you were present and absent at the same time. And now I am here with you. Does that mean I am also here and back at Dunvegan as well?" he mused, talking out the situation before them.

"Is such a thing possible?" Rosalyn asked.

Keiran nodded. "In a dream state, aye."

She drew a sharp breath. "Oberon mentioned that if I died in my dreams I would die in life. So, all of this is a dream?"

"A dream where there are deadly consequences if we fail." Keiran's gaze dropped to the map. "Let us look at what we are up against, shall we?"

The map had been fashioned on aged parchment, making it appear as though from ancient times. The inscribed coastline around Dunvegan was obvious to Keiran and would have been even before he could read. Around the geographical outline of the coastline, rivers, harbours, and forests, were colourful images of fairies.

"This is more a work of art than a directional tool," Keiran said in frustration. There were no place names, no writing whatsoever. "If Oberon gave us this challenge because I could not read, then why not have words on the page?"

"Perhaps that is what he wants us to believe," Rosalyn said, as she began to see certain patterns repeating in the design of the fairies. By folding the map in one place, she brought two of the patterns together. A letter started to form. Her heart soared. Perhaps they might outwit the trickster yet. "We must fold these images on the map."

"Oberon would not make it that simple for us."

Still, Keiran studied the map, and while he did, Rosalyn shifted her gaze to the hourglass Oberon had left behind. One-fourth of the sand had already drifted downward. "Time is slipping away."

"Our worrying about that will not help us keep our wits about us," Keiran said, then raised his gaze to hers. "I have an idea. Look at the compass rose on the map. It shows the four cardinal directions. Perhaps we try folding the parchment like that."

Rosalyn began folding the paper, aligning her folds with the needle of the compass specifying true north as their landmark. When no words appeared, she frowned and unfolded the map. "What other landmarks on this map can we use?"

Keiran searched the area. "Orrick told me there are two

waterfalls near here. Is there any indication of them on the map?"

"No, only rock formations," she said with frustration. Fiona was counting on them to figure this out and protect her unborn baby.

Keiran tapped two fingers over the rock formation of Castle Ewen. "Fold the map with this as the landmark."

"Look, letters start to appear!" Rosalyn frowned. "But they do not make any sense."

"Try folding it again using an eight-point compass rose with the four cardinal directions and the four intercardinal directions," Keiran suggested.

As she folded, her excitement grew. Letters started to form. They were written in a fashion that reminded her of old English scripts she had seen in some of the older books she had read from her brother's library. They often had an initial letter at the beginning of the chapter that was bold and ornate. She could make out the letter L, then as she kept folding a V appeared, followed by an E, and finally an O. "Love." Her shoulders slumped. "That is not much of a clue."

Keiran frowned and reached for the map. He turned the folded parchment upside down and now the word read Pain.

"It is an ambigram. These words are so ornate, they can form two different things when looked at from two different directions."

Rosalyn released a frustrated breath. "How does that help

us?"

Keiran pointed to the map again. To the faint X that showed on not one, but two places a short distance from them. "I will speculate these represent two waterfalls. I would wager he has hidden her behind one of them."

Rosalyn looked back at the hourglass. Time in the form of sand slipped through faster than she would have liked.

Striding to the hourglass, Keiran tried to set it on its side, to slow time for them, but the timepiece would not budge. "If we cannot stop time, then we will simply have to find her in the time allowed."

"But, I mean, 'pain?' That word scares me, Keiran, for both of us."

"Do not lose hope simply because one of the words Oberon used as a clue was pain. Aye, we have both had our fair share of disappointments in our lives, but we are not the same people we once were." He pulled her close, holding on to her as if they had all the time in the world. That sizzle of heat she always experienced when they touched passed between them. "We will defeat Oberon if we stand together."

She tipped her head back to look up at him. "We do this together."

He released her and took her hand as they headed through a sea of green hillsides for the waterfalls in the distance.

"You said there are two? How will we know which waterfall to search?" Together they clambered down a steep incline.

Keiran sighed heavily. "Oberon expects us to split up, to each search one. That we will not do because I am certain that will lead us to the pain part of Oberon's message. We make a choice and pray it is the correct one in our allotted time left."

From the path, they could see both waterfalls and two trails leading in separate directions. At the end of one path was a large waterfall, with rushing water that flowed into a stream that joined with the water from the second smaller waterfall. "Which will we choose? The larger one, or the smaller one?"

"Oberon would believe we would choose the larger, so I say we head towards the smaller one," Keiran offered, guiding them in that direction.

A seed of doubt lingered inside Rosalyn. She stopped, forcing Keiran to do the same. "Or does he think that is what we will expect him to do, so he will do the opposite? And we will find Fiona behind the larger waterfall?"

Keiran's expression turned grim. "One of us has to make this decision and both of us will live with the outcome, whether good or bad."

Rosalyn swallowed roughly. "This is the pain portion of Oberon's message. A choice we must make to save or lose someone we love."

"Since you were the focus of Oberon's revenge against

me and the MacLeods, it makes sense that he would gear this choice towards your logic instead of mine. I trust you, Rosalyn. Let us follow the path towards the larger waterfall." He brought her hand to his lips and kissed her fingertips. "Our past is gone. All we have now is the present. And our future awaits if we can claim it after this madness is through."

Staring into his brown eyes, she felt his belief in her and clung to it. "We will."

They took the path to the left. As they approached the waterfall the muted sound of rushing water filled the air. They turned a bend in the path and came to a rock face with a waterfall snuggled into its side. The grey shale surrounding the waterfall glistened with spray. Foamy water tumbled downward, splashing noisily into a naturally made pool that then flowed into the stream beyond.

Looking beyond the beauty of the setting, Rosalyn frowned. "I do not see Fiona."

"Oberon would not make her easy to find." Keiran nodded towards the water. "We will have to go through the falls, and hope there is a hidden cave behind the water where she waits for us. Come."

Her thoughts moved back to the hourglass for a moment before she tightened her grip on Keiran's hand and followed him into the water. They waded waist deep before they were forced to release their grip on each other and swim through the plunge pool.

"Ready?" Keiran asked as they approached the falls.

Rosalyn nodded and, holding her breath dove beneath the splash, praying for an undercut with air to breathe on the opposite side.

When she came up, Rosalyn was overjoyed to see an open space in the hazy light. She drew a deep breath and searched for Keiran. He was not beside her any longer. She searched the water behind her, then dove beneath the water to see he had become trapped by something on his way into the cave.

Nothing.

Rosalyn dove again and again as fear snaked through her. Where was he? Because he wasn't below the water. She broke through the water again and searched the cave. He would not have had time to get out of the water before her, would he? Her heart soared when she saw a shadowy figure on the small shelf behind the waterfall. As the figure crept towards her, she cried out, "Fiona!" Relief flooded her even as her desperation to find Keiran left her raw and aching. Oberon had made finding the young woman not difficult once she and Keiran had chosen the right path.

Love and pain, Oberon's message had been to them. Tears came to Rosalyn's eyes as the love in her heart swelled, momentarily assuaging her fear at Keiran's absence. She had loved Keiran from the moment she had first looked into his eyes as she lay dying. And in that moment, it did not really matter if she could love him every day for the next year, or if

GERRI RUSSELL

she were lucky enough to love him for the rest of her life. She would take what joy she could and cling to it for as long as he would let her.

Then another idea occurred to her as she scrambled onto the ledge where Fiona perched. "It is glad I am to see you safe."

"You came for me," Fiona said with a tremor in her voice. "I tried to leave this place myself, but I cannot swim."

"It does not matter," Rosalyn said slowly. Oberon somehow had known that. Oberon knew many things. And Oberon was a trickster. Rosalyn looked down at Fiona's arm and noticed the absence of her bracelet. Had Oberon tricked them all into removing the protection of the silver they had worn? Rosalyn's eyes narrowed for a moment, but then she gave a little rallying shake of her head, and added, "I believe I know how we can get out of this place, but I will need you to trust me."

Fiona nodded, relief sparking in her gaze. "I do trust you."

Rosalyn pressed her lips into a thin line. "I apologise for what I am about to do to you, Fiona. Believe me, it is necessary." Rosalyn brought her hand up, and slapped Fiona hard across the cheek.

Fiona gasped and her eyes went wide. She brought her hand up to cover her cheek, and in the next moment, she faded away.

Rosalyn allowed herself a quick grin before she jumped

back into the pool of water and swam to the other side of the waterfall. Fiona was only partially in this magical in-between place Oberon had taken them to. From what Keiran had told her about her own body frozen in time in the old keep, she had determined that only by causing Fiona pain would the woman wake from her enchanted slumber and be right where she belonged, back at Dunvegan.

Rosalyn broke through the surface of the water on the other side of the plunge pool, hoping beyond hope that she might see Keiran. But he was nowhere in sight. Oberon must have taken him while they had been under the water, relocating him somewhere else in this strange in-between place. What other explanation was there for Keiran's absence when he had been right beside her not long ago?

They had played Oberon's game and had found Fiona, yet Rosalyn could not really say they had won because now Oberon had taken Keiran from her. "Oberon, you have reneged on your promise to send us home."

The hourglass suddenly appeared at her feet, the sand frozen in place, reflecting that she'd beat the fairy king's timeline. "Where is Keiran?"

A breeze suddenly kicked up behind Rosalyn, pushing her along the path she and Keiran had taken before. Rosalyn did not fight the wind. Instead, she let it carry her along until she was back in the Fairy Glen, heading towards Castle Ewen, where the wind died as quickly as it had come.

Ahead of her Castle Ewen dominated the landscape.

That was where she would find Keiran. She did not know how she knew this, but she did. Perhaps some of Keiran's fairy-touched nature was rubbing off on her?

She steeled herself for what came next. It was time to take a stand against Oberon or he would continue to pursue Keiran, and all the MacLeods. They would never know a moment's peace.

Rosalyn broke into a run. A part of her soul had died along with her parents, and half her heart had died in a Scottish forest—then Keiran had entered her life. And something new had grown inside her, something she never wanted to turn away from again.

She was no longer afraid.

CHAPTER TWENTY-TWO

K EIRAN TRIED TO cry out when he saw Rosalyn climbing the rock formation that made up Castle Ewen. Besides any treacherousness of the climb, he had to warn her of Oberon's presence. Except, every sound he made was caught and carried away by the wind. And every movement he made caused Oberon to tighten the invisible hold he had on Keiran that felt like an iron band around his chest, squeezing the very life from his body.

Oberon had snatched him away from Rosalyn as they had dived under the falls. He prayed she had been successful in her quest to find Fiona. He only wished she had stayed safely away from the one man determined to crush any dream they had of happiness together.

"Welcome, my dear," Oberon greeted Rosalyn when she appeared at the top of the rock formation. The surface was flat and wide, making it far less dangerous than the other rock she had been on in the middle of the churning sea. But just like that rock, the wind caught her hair, sending it fluttering about her face.

"Release him, Oberon," Rosalyn said, her tone even and

steady. "We played your game and found Fiona."

"Nonsense." Oberon laughed. "You beat the hourglass, but this game goes on until I say it is finished."

Rosalyn walked slowly towards him. "You think you are all-powerful, toying with people's lives as you do. You are not brave like Keiran. Only a weak man manipulates others to make himself feel bigger, stronger, more in control. How does any creature in Fairyland take you seriously as a king, as a leader? As a father, as a man? Or are they all so afraid of you that they fall in line with whatever you want? No wonder you are so bored in Fairyland and find ways to escape into the human realm to amuse yourself."

Anger blazed across Oberon's features. "You know nothing about me or my people."

"Perhaps not, but you know nothing of humans either. Not really," Rosalyn said. "Did you know that in the human realm there are stories written about you, songs sung to you? Human fascination with fairies reflects our own yearning for a world that is magical and wondrous."

Oberon's anger lessened as curiosity crept into his eyes.

Keiran's own curiosity had been piqued, not by Oberon, but by the strong, brave, wonderful woman who kept moving slowly towards him.

"Humans are an interesting lot," Rosalyn told him. "What they once glorify can later so easily be tarnished. If I were to write a story, a song, or even a play that portrays you as a poor loser who is also foolish, unintelligent, clumsy, frivolous, and ignorant, humans might start to believe they were wrong before and that all those new traits are the truth about you, and possibly all fairies."

"I would never allow such." Oberon speared Rosalyn with a hard stare.

Rosalyn shrugged. "You would not have any control over the situation. You are a fairy. You rule Fairyland, not the human realm."

Keiran had to hold back a smile at how extraordinarily composed she appeared. "Tales of misdeeds and faults travel fast in the human realm, more so than virtues," Keiran added.

Oberon's eyes flared with fear. The wind kicked up, howling, swirling around the three of them atop the castle formation.

"What if I gifted you with power?" Oberon said, his voice tentative. "What if I asked you both to join me in Fairyland, and allowed you to rule over one of the lands? Think of the dynasty we could build together."

Rosalyn shifted her gaze to Keiran and in the depths of her eyes he read her plea to trust him.

He returned an almost imperceptible nod as she stopped beside Oberon and within an arm's reach of Keiran.

"Your world, your magic does not interest me. The only thing I want—all I have ever wanted is Keiran. I love you," she said moving to him and wrapping her arms around him.

"And I love you," Keiran replied, drawing a deep breath

as suddenly the band around his chest vanished.

"No!" Oberon's shriek of fury pierced the air and travelled with them as they vanished from the Fairy Glen and found themselves once more in the secret passageway of the old keep.

Keiran pulled Rosalyn into his arms and held her tight. "I have never seen Oberon terrified before. Your threat of rewriting his legacy truly shook him to his core. I cannot say we have seen the last of Oberon, though I very much doubt he will interfere in our lives anytime soon thanks to you."

Rosalyn grinned up at him, and he felt the sweet rush of peace break through him. "I was terrified when you vanished from the pool under the waterfall."

"Did you find Fiona?"

"Yes, and I sent her home."

"How?"

"The message Oberon gave us: love and pain. I figured that was the key to leaving the in-between place where Oberon took us. I unfortunately tested my theory on Fiona, causing her temporary pain. When she vanished before my eyes, I knew that for us to be set free of Oberon's trap we had to finally declare what was in our hearts."

Keiran closed his eyes, letting the moment register so that he would always be able to recall the instant he no longer felt anything but human. He might still have healing powers, but those would be used to protect the safety and well-being of his clan, against the English and Oberon in the future should the need arise.

The fairy king had not been fully conquered. He could still make mischief in their world, and for the MacLeods. But if the MacLeods had learned anything in the past several days, it was that the members of their family had skills and abilities above his own that could help them defeat the fairy king should he dare to meddle in their lives again.

Keiran opened his eyes and smiled down at the woman in his arms. "We have both been through so much in the past few days. When we handfasted, the terms of our joining were for only a year and a day. So much has changed since we made that promise to each other. Now, I cannot bear the thought of being apart from you, not even for a moment. You are the most amazing woman I have ever known. You are a survivor. You are intelligent. You are witty. You are beautiful. And I love you."

Rosalyn drew a sharp breath and looked at him with longing in her eyes. "I am the woman who loves you more than life. I want, more than anything, to spend every day of the rest of my life with you."

Keiran took Rosalyn's face in his hands and kissed her with the promise of forever between them. "What do you say if we change the terms of our agreement?"

"What did you have in mind?"

"Will eternity be long enough for you?"

Her smile faltered. "Everything inside me longs to say yes. How do I know I am free to make that commitment?"

"Heavens, in all the excitement, I forgot to tell you that Lieutenant Long accepted our offer of a promotion and to leave you in peace. You are free to do with your life whatever you choose, Rosalyn."

"Then I choose life with you, Keiran. For as long as you will have me."

Before he could answer, a frothy grey mist swept into the passageway, then gathered into a more solid shape until the image of Lady Janet appeared before them.

You have returned to us. Everyone will be so pleased. Come, she urged them to follow her out of the passageway. *Everyone has been waiting for days to see you safe again.*

"Days?" Rosalyn asked, her expression one of confusion. "How is that possible? It seemed like such a short time while we were there."

Keiran took Rosalyn's hand in his and together they headed for the front courtyard. "Somehow that doesn't surprise me. Time in other realms passes differently than it does in the human realm." They exited the old keep and had to shield their eyes for a moment as their vision adjusted to the brightness of the spring afternoon. The air was crisp and clean, carrying the scent of wildflowers and the tang of the sea. The sun above was bright, though not yet warm as it bathed the courtyard in a gentle glow.

At the sight of the gaping hole in the castle wall, Rosalyn's steps slowed. "What happened here?"

"Nothing that cannot be fixed." His bride had been frozen and half in another realm while the attack had happened, unable to know what occurred in their home. Keiran noted that the men had cleared the entire courtyard of rubble, and that repairs had already started on the missing piece of the wall.

As they continued towards the new keep, the door of the castle burst open and Fiona and Tormod were the first to emerge, followed by the rest of the MacLeod clan. They filled the courtyard with excited voices and cheers of celebration that Keiran and Rosalyn had returned.

Fiona greeted Rosalyn with a hug. When Rosalyn opened her mouth to speak, Fiona held up her hand, cutting her off. "I do not want to hear an apology. You did not hurt me." She offered Rosalyn a view of her smooth cheek. "You sent me back here, where I belong, and where you belong."

Tormod pulled Fiona into his arms. "You have my thanks as well, Rosalyn. I went mad when Fiona disappeared, and I could not find her. If you ever need anything at all, please let me know. We are indebted to you, dear sister."

Rosalyn blinked back tears. "I do not know what to say."

Keiran's entire family gathered around them. "Say you will stay with us and be the Scottish lass you were always meant to be," Tormod said with a wink.

Rosalyn turned her gaze to Keiran's. "I did not want to be a Scot when I first arrived here. Now I want nothing more."

As Keiran stared into her hazel eyes, the world around

them faded into the background, until there was only the two of them.

"I have thoughts, but why do you think Oberon used the words *love* and *pain* on the map he left for us?" Rosalyn asked him.

"Perhaps because instead of opposites, they are one and the same. To love, one must risk feeling pain, hurt, vulnerability, and even the possibility of loss," Keiran mused.

He reached for Rosalyn and pulled her close. "Outweighing all that is finding a place where both you and I belong and are surrounded by those who love us." He brought his lips to her ear. "Not to mention the thrill of being in your true love's arms at the end of each day."

A smile swept across her face. "Is that what I am to you? Your true love?"

"Always and forever. I love you, Rosalyn." Hope for their future filled his heart to bursting.

She reached up and brushed a lock of his hair away from his face. "And I love you, Keiran MacLeod."

He brought his lips to hers to seal their declaration, this time for a lifetime. His hands caressed her back and the spark that was ever-present between them flared. Would it always be like that between them? His healing touch moving into her and her sending it back to him? He hoped so, as he continued to kiss her with gentle thoroughness.

Caught in the joy of kissing her, Keiran did not hear the roar around him at first. But as he released her lips to draw her against his side, the full force of Clan MacLeod cheered around them.

Rosalyn rested her head on his chest and smiled. "I have a family who loves me and a husband I adore. Does life get any better than this?"

He returned her smile. "I suspect it gets better, much better. And I intend to show you just how much as soon as we are alone."

Rosalyn laughed, the sound warm and seductive, as she nestled closer.

Keiran drew a satisfied breath. It had only taken nine years, but he was finally where he belonged. Home, at Dunvegan with his family, and with the woman he loved wrapped in his arms. Through the peaks and valleys in their future, love, not pain, would be their constant star, guiding them towards a life overflowing with every good thing they ever imagined.

THE END

AUTHOR'S NOTE

Skye is the largest and northernmost major island of the Inner Hebrides. Wing-shaped and deeply indented by sea lochs, it fans out from the western coast of the Scottish mainland towards the outer islands of the Hebridean archipelago. It is not hard to believe magical things can happen among the giant escarpments, needle-like pinnacles, and mist-shrouded mountains that tower over shimmering lochs and wild moors.

Hidden in the hills of Uig, is an enchanting geological formation called the Fairy Glen (*Bail nan cnoc* in Gaelic, meaning the village in the hills) that Rosalyn and Keiran visit in *Enchanted by the Highlander*. This magical area has a reputation for being a place of myth and wonder. The Fairy Glen was formed over hundred thousand years ago by post-glacier landslides, while years of erosion and the elements sculpted the Torridonian sandstone into unusual patterns of cone-shaped craggy hillocks, random boulders, tranquil lochans, and even a basalt castle. Visitors to the area often leave rocks in circle formations around the glen, making it easy to believe that fairies live there.

Travels into Several Remote Nations of the World. In Four

Parts. By Lemuel Gulliver, First a Surgeon, and then a Captain of Several Ships by Jonathan Swift was published anonymously in October of 1726 and was an instant best seller, selling over ten thousand copies in the first three weeks. The book later became known as *Gulliver's Travels* and was one of the first fantasy novels ever published.

If you enjoyed *Enchanted by the Highlander*,
you'll love the other books in the...

GUARDIANS OF THE ISLES SERIES

Book 1: *The Return of the Heir*

Book 2: *Only a Highlander Will Do*

Book 3: *To Win a Highlander's Heart*

Book 4: *To Claim His Highland Bride*

Book 5: *A Little Highland Magic*

Book 6: Enchanted by the Highlander

Available now at your favorite online retailer!

A special preview from the final book in the
Guardians of the Isles series,
Taming the Highland Beauty

THE LAUGHTER OF Clan MacLeod drifted through the salt-laden air as Gille looked on from the back of the crowd gathered to welcome Rosalyn and Keiran home from whatever adventure they had been on for the past two days. Gille smiled as she caught a glimpse of Rosalyn and Keiran emerging from the old keep, unharmed. These two had overcome so many obstacles, even death, to be together in this life.

With her next breath, a pang of longing pierced her. How she craved to belong to a family as Rosalyn now did, as Aria had before her. Perhaps, there was hope for Gille in the future to be a part of a clan like the MacLeods.

Suddenly, a cold hand clamped over her shoulder. Gille gasped, whirling around to find Oberon, his face twisted in a cruel smile. "Enjoying the festivities, little traitor?" His voice dripped with amusement.

Panic flooded Gille as memories of her attempt to destroy the fairy king in Fairyland flashed before her. "Your Majesty. I meant you no harm," she stammered.

"No harm?" Oberon tilted his head, searching her face. "You sought to kill me. You sent me into the shadow realm." He raised his hand, and a malevolent green light pulsed from his fingertips. Pain flared in Gille's chest. A coiling sensation tightened around her heart. Frantically, she looked at the others. To see if anyone noticed Oberon's presence. But they all simply laughed and talked to each other as though nothing untoward was happening in their presence.

"They cannot see you. Not any longer," Oberon said with an evil smile. "Since you almost destroyed me, I will curse you, Gille. You shall live the rest of your days alone in the woodlands of the human realm," Oberon declared. "The joy you so desperately crave shall forever remain just beyond your grasp."

"Nay," Gille cried out.

"Since I am not a monster, I will allow you to leave the woodlands for a short time—seven days, but no longer—just long enough for you to remember what you are missing. If you do not make it back to the forest before sunset on the seventh day, you will turn into a tree." The light intensified, tendrils of it wrapping around Gille, tearing at the very fabric of her being. Then as abruptly as it began, it was over.

Gille slumped to the ground at the base of an old, moss-covered beech tree, finding herself not at Dunvegan, but in the woodlands beyond. She could still hear laughter coming from the castle, but it now sounded like a distant, mocking echo. She was truly alone, condemned to wander the woodlands, yearning for a happiness that could never be hers.

More books by Gerri Russell

All the Kings Men series

Book 1: *Seven Nights with a Scot*

Book 2: *Romancing the Laird*

Book 3: *A Temptress in Tartan*

Book 4: *A Laird and a Gentleman*

Book 5: *Much Ado About a Scot*

Available now at your favorite online retailer!

About the Author

Barbara Roser Photography

Gerri Russell is the award-winning author of historical and contemporary novels including the Brotherhood of the Scottish Templars series and *Flirting with Felicity*. A two-time recipient of the Romance Writers of America's Golden Heart Award and winner of the American Title II competition sponsored by *RT Book Reviews* magazine, she is best known for her adventurous and emotionally intense novels set in the thirteenth- and fourteenth-century Scottish Highlands. Before Gerri followed her passion for writing romance novels, she worked as a broadcast journalist, a newspaper reporter, a magazine columnist, a technical writer and editor, and an instructional designer. She lives in the Pacific Northwest with her husband and four mischievous black cats.

Thank you for reading

ENCHANTED BY THE HIGHLANDER

If you enjoyed this book, you can find more from all our great authors at TulePublishing.com, or from your favorite online retailer.

TULE
PUBLISHING

Made in the USA
Coppell, TX
12 February 2025